The Irish Match

The Irish Match

('Tis a fine Tail)

STEVE PARKER

iUniverse, Inc.
Bloomington

The Irish Match
('Tis a fine Tail)

iUniverse books may be ordered through booksellers or by contacting:

iUniverse
1663 Liberty Drive
Bloomington, IN 47403
www.iuniverse.com
1-800-Authors (1-800-288-4677)

Because of the dynamic nature of the Internet, any web addresses or links contained in this book may have changed since publication and may no longer be valid. The views expressed in this work are solely those of the author and do not necessarily reflect the views of the publisher, and the publisher hereby disclaims any responsibility for them.

Any people depicted in stock imagery provided by Thinkstock are models, and such images are being used for illustrative purposes only.
Certain stock imagery © Thinkstock.

ISBN: 978-1-4759-7358-7 (sc)
ISBN: 978-1-4759-7359-4 (ebk)

Library of Congress Control Number: 2013901472

Printed in the United States of America

iUniverse rev. date: 01/23/2013

Dedication

This magnificent work is dedicated to John M. Rowley, a fine wreck of a man, and John A. Carter, the boy who put the cock in cockney.

Warning . . . if you are easily offended by profanities
and sexual innuendo please, read no further . . .

Prologue

"Holy Mary and Joseph will ya look at this!" said Liam Duff, pushing his peaked cap to the back of his head, and spreading out two 20 punt notes side by side on the counter of the bank.

"Look at what?" asked Eamon Duff, Liam's brother and co-director of 'DUFF SECURITY'.

"They're identical!" exclaimed Liam.

"Of course they are ya daft eejit," said Eamon, "they're both 20 punt notes."

"No, Eamon, I mean, they are IDENTICAL! Look at the serial numbers!" said Liam. Eamon looked closely at the two Irish banknotes.

"Feck me!" he said, "we must 'phone the Garda. One of dems a fake!"

Liam rubbed the palm of his hand across his forehead and stared vacantly for a few moments.

"We will not," he said.

"Have ya gone barmy man?" said Eamon, "'tis the fraud you're looking at here!"

"Look," said Liam, "what have we to do with these banknotes now, Eamon?"

"Well," said Eamon, "they've been sprayed with the pink dye, so we've just to take them to Dublin for the burning."

"That's right," said Liam, "and if a few clever bog-trotters are now Euro-millionaires, who gives a shite? Good luck to them. The government can afford it. Jesus, we're the richest country in Europe!"

"I don't get it," said Eamon.

"Ireland is on schedule to be 100% 'Euro' by the end of the month," said Liam, "and I'll not be lettin' this," Liam pointed to the twin banknotes, "upset the feckin' applecart and make us look like a bunch of thick 'Micks'!"

"Sure and you've a point there," said Eamon.

"Keep it under your hat," said Liam seriously.

Eamon looked from side to side and then quickly took both of the notes and put them under his hat.

The Team

The team consists of four course fishermen, Sid, Dave, Jonah and Rowley. They are members of their local pub's fishing club, The Spit and Sawdust, Freshfield, Liverpool. They are, quite simply, the best rod and line fishermen in N.W. England (or so they would like people to believe). The area-final was to be held the following weekend. Win it and they would be in the big one! Five days in Ireland for the 'All England Rod and Line Championship' and a first prize of 100,000 Euros, with huge sponsorship spin offs.

(1) 'Dirty' Sid Lennon 35 divorced. Electrician. Born: Fazakerley, Liverpool. 6ft 2in. Not too fastidious on the personal hygiene stakes. Has halitosis. Is slim with dark, lank hair and a permanent 7 O'clock shadow. He's a bit of a joker, and an erstwhile ladies man. Hobbies:—Fishing, karaoke singing and sex.

(2) Dave Tonks 22 single. Tyler. Born: Gateacre Liverpool. 6ft 4in. Immeasurably thick. He has a shock of red hair and a massive frame festooned with freckles (and boils). Strange lad is Dave. Hobbies:—Fishing, growing boils, odd wanking.

(3) Jonah Carter 30 single. Car Salesman. Born Muswell Hill, London. 5ft 8in and a real-life 'Jack the Lad'. Good looking, wiry, fit and cocky with it. Hobbies:—Sex, fishing, sex, money, sex, cars and sex.

(4) J.P. Rowley 50 married 4 kids. Teacher. Born: Hanley Stoke-on-Trent. 5ft 11in athletic build rapidly going to seed. Fair complexion. Completely bald. Hobbies:—Fishing, assessing the merits of tits, dreaming of retiring.

And so on with the tale . . .

Chapter 1

"I'm related to John Lennon, y'know," said 'dirty' Sid, positioning an in-ceiling light fitment into a huge new bathroom in an extremely 'des res' on the outskirts of Southport.

"Oh, go on," replied Mrs. Wainwright, of 46 Willowbay Crescent, Birkdale. A very tidy 30-something who just couldn't stop looking at 'dirty' Sid Lennon's crotch.

"Oh, yeah s'true," said Sid, "Er, Freddie Lennon, y'know, John's dad, was my dad's second cousin, er, once removed, I think," and Sid laughed.

"Gerraway," said Audrey Wainwright, "You're pullin' me leg."

"No 'onest," said Sid, lying unconvincingly, "mind you if there's any pullin' to do you could try this," and Sid cupped his lunchbox in his hand and gave it a suggestive tug.

"Oh you are awful," said Audrey.

"But I like you," replied Sid instantly, and they both burst out laughing.

"Find this a home," said Sid, still gripping his crotch, "and the 10% discount is 15%, okay?"

Audrey flushed, bit her lower lip, looked at her watch and took a deep breath.

"Oh, go on then, you smooth talking bastard!"

'Dirty' Sid Lennon shagged the living daylights out of Audrey Wainwright and gave her 15% discount instead of the usual 10%. As an added bonus, he also gave her an embarrassing dose of genital herpes. Never too fastidious about removing the cream cheese from under his foreskin was our Sid. He also suffered from bad breath, halitosis, and continually wondered why people invariably offered him Polos or Extra Strong Mints. Poor old 'dirty' Sid.

Sid drove out of Willowbay Crescent, his last job of the day, and headed for his local, 'The Spit and Sawdust' in Freshfield.

Whereas most 20-odd year old men would be out chasing women, or at least pump their peckers looking at 'girlie' magazines or video porn, Dave Tonks didn't. Dave was different. The cheese had certainly slid off Dave's cracker long ago.

Dave had a huge head, and when he struggled into the world 22 years previously in Liverpool Maternity Hospital, there was more than a suggestion of oxygen deprivation. Dave's mum after the painful trauma of birth and on seeing her first ugly sibling promptly opted for anal sex for the rest of her reproductive life. Nonetheless, Dave grew to be 6ft 4in tall and was not too bad looking apart from his acne. This had arrived with a vengeance when Dave was 13 and still festooned his features almost a decade later. Dave also grew monumental boils. He would nurture them like painful pulsating volcanoes and, when he judged the time was right, would lance them with a hot sewing needle. He would then squeeze the blooded pus out leaving an unsightly spent crater to further adorn his infected skin.

Dave was fanatical about fishing. He was also brilliant at it. If there was only one roach in a 15-acre lake, Dave Tonks could catch it. The only English he truly understood was what was written in fishing magazines. He studied them all the time, usually accompanied by a rock-solid hard-on. Yes, Dave was indeed, different. The moment he hooked and started playing a large fish, Dave would sprout an instant erection. Dave wanked looking at photographs of large carp.

"F'fuck's sake Dave, will you put that fuckin' fishin' magazine away? Hump up some fuckin' tiles so we can finish this fuckin' roof before fuckin' Christmas!"

bellowed Dave's articulate boss, Mike Gobb, who was precariously balancing on a two inch wide wooden lath, on top of a roofless council house in Speke.

"Ah right, ah right, calm down, calm down," said Dave, stuffing his copy of 'Improve Your Freshwater Fishing', into the arse pocket of his faded Levis, perching a dozen roof tiles on his right shoulder and shinnying up a wobbly metal ladder up to the roof.

Mike Gobb had a soft spot for Dave and, having taken him on when he left school, had taught him his trade. Mike also had a soft spot (well, a hard one really) for Dave's Mum, whom he serviced regularly. Mike could never figure out why Dave's Mum preferred sex in trap 2. His own missus would never allow anal sex. Mike smiled at the thought, slipped off the wooden lath, and, as soon as his right leg ripped through the asphalt sheeting, the rest of him promptly followed.

Dave peered through the hole in the roof and saw his boss looking up at him flat out on the floor of a council house loft.

"You ain't done that for ages," said Dave.

"Fuck off!" said Mike.

Dave fucked off to 'The Spit and Sawdust'.

"I tell you sonninck," Jonah Carter's unmistakable London accent, "you're on a winner with this Ford Zetec." J.A. Carter made Del-boy Trotter look like a novice.

"Full service history, (written by Carter) average to low mileage, (clocked from 89000 to 26000 by Carter), here have a butcher's at this!" Jonah Carter whipped out the latest edition of 'Parker's Guide to Used Car Prices' and leafed through to the 'Ford' section. "The punter's bible, what can I say, here it is;—'One year old Ford Zetec 1.8 LX 5-door, alloys, metallic paint, FSH, low mileage. Look at the recommended price, and you can have it for over a grand less!" Jonah then pointed to a row of Fords from Galaxies to Fiestas.

"See this lot? Bankrupt stock, got them for a song didn't I? The savings are past on to the customer. Brilliant model this. Yours for seven and three daughters (£7750). Now can I say fairer than that?" The punter was genuinely impressed.

"Tell you what, I'll even throw in a years tax and a 3 month warranty gratis. What do you think?" and Jonah smiled.

The punter was hooked, and Jonah had sold his fifth shed that morning. The convinced punter signed a debilitating credit agreement and drove off smiling in his shiny Ford Zetec, which was destined to be a complete MOT failure six months later.

Jonah beamed gratuitously his hands thrust deep into his pockets and, rocking on the heels of his expensive Italian shoes, turned to his boss George Higgins and declared, "I'm a fackin' diamond in I George?"

"Jonah, you could sell video-games to the blind!" said George.

"Too true my son, too true . . . here watch this!" Jonah had spotted a middle-aged couple drooling over a cocked-up-insurance-right-off-Rover 75.

"Piece of fackin' cake" said Jonah, and he stubbed out his expensive gold-tipped ciggie under the heel of his expensive Italian shoe and was off to secure his sixth sale before lunch.

Jonah Carter had worked for George Higgins for the past 4 years, and had completely turned around his ailing second hand car business. Jonah had connections at every car auctions in the U.K. and bought, on average, 20 cars a week. He never bid on a single car. He simply slipped the auctioneer £50 for every car he had earmarked and, despite the bidding, the chosen car was knocked down to 'Higgins Autos Merseyside' and released at the reserve price or lower. Curiously, Jonah never went to any car auctions in the London area. The reason for this was the value Jonah placed on his hide, or, more precisely, his genitals. Jonah was lying low.

Jonah, the boy who put the cock in cockney, was a marked man. Four years previously in London, Jonah was excelling at his three favorite pursuits;—1. Fishing, 2. Selling cars, and 3. Putting his huge cock into every available female orifice he could smarm into bed.

"Spanking the flaps!" was his term for sex. Flap spanking was his undoing. He only did it for a bet.

"With the tackle I've got," said Carter, heartily cupping his meat and two veg through his expensive designer strides, "and my inherent Cockney charm, I could poke any bird I wanted!"

"Bet you couldn't poke Mrs. Hoskins," said Benny Miles, Jonah's fishing-cum-drinking partner.

"How much?" said a confident Carter.

"You wouldn't dare! The boss's missus! He'd have your guts for garters, you barmy bastard."

"How much then, my son?"

"You serious?"

"Must be worth a ton, Benny old son."

"You're fackin' mental!"

Nevertheless, they shook on it.

Jonah duly charmed himself into Glenda Hoskins' knickers with Benny Miles atop a ladder at the bedroom window, ogling Jonah Carter's undulating bum, as he pushed every millimetre of his 9-inch donger into the grateful Glenda. When he was down to the short strokes, Jonah couldn't help giggling to himself, as he looked at the bedside photograph of Charlie Hoskins, his boss. Charlie was holding a huge carp with the inscription:—'S.E. London Area Champion'.

"Fackin' amateur Charlie," Jonah said to himself, as Charlie himself sauntered into the bedroom! Benny became the vanishing voyeur, Charlie went ballistic and Jonah's survival instincts went into overdrive.

As Charlie went for Jonah's jugular, Jonah rammed a bedside cabinet into Charlie's shins, flung open the window and slid down Benny's ladder. Jonah raced off stark-bollock naked and terrified into the Chelsea night.

Charlie Hoskins vowed that once he caught up with cocky Carter he would reduce his wedding-tackle to a 1-inch stump. And he would.

Jonah disappeared, surfaced on Merseyside and went to work for George Higgins.

Jonah was so good at his job; he worked on his own terms. £200 per day and £200 for every car sold. Cash in hand, no tax, no cards no paperwork and unpaid time off for Jonah to indulge in his passion . . . fishing. George Higgins's boat had come in.

Today Jonah had earned £1800. He was off to 'The Spit and Sawdust'.

James Paul Rowley was an outstanding science teacher and fisherman. He could and should have made a good head teacher, but he loathed the administrative side of his profession and was always happiest at 'the chalk face'. He breezed to a double first in Chemistry at Liverpool University and was top of the pile on acquiring his PGCE, his classroom persona ascribed by a single word, 'brilliant'. At Liverpool he had met and married Trish, a throwback to the halcyon days of hippies, the avante garde, pot smoking, vegetarianism and the Beatles.

More by luck than judgment Rowley was appointed Head of Science in a huge Liverpool Comprehensive. The school had the best chemistry 'A' level results in the city and was in the top 10 nationwide, thanks to Rowley. Strangely, no one ever used his Christian names; everyone called him 'Rowley'.

However, since reaching the age of 50, some of the professional spark had gone and Rowley found himself daydreaming about retiring and spending more time fishing. He hated writing lesson-plans but was duty bound to lead his department by example.

"Why the bollocks am I writing this when I've a thousand lessons indelibly printed in my brain?" he said to himself. Rowley talked to himself all the time.

Rowley and Trish had produced 4 children in 6 years, Fleur, Abigail, Dougal and Jake. Trish loved being pregnant. She would caress her lump and call herself 'earth-mother' during each confinement. She would have been content to spawn a football team, with reserves. Rowley saw the writing on the wall in the guise of his ever-increasing overdraft. He feigned influenza for a week, slid off to the local clinic and had a 'snip-job'. He suffered ball-ache for two weeks and never sired any more siblings. He never told Trish. On their 10th anniversary, Trish had arranged for them to be 'tested' to ascertain, why no more babies had arrived. Rowley agreed, and when it was announced that his sperm count was zero, Trish became closer and more loving towards him. This suited Rowley, just fine.

The bell rang to end afternoon break. Rowley had two lessons left to deliver. Year 7 'collision theory of reacting particles' and the lower 6th, 'Periodic Table:—The Transition Elements.' Rowley had a student in tow from the local college, Sarah Taylor. The student was in awe of Rowley, having seen him teach several times; she also had nice tits, which suited Rowley just fine.

"Come on then Sarah, (wiggle your tits over here)" said Rowley.

"Let's go and stun this Year 7 class {or would you like to be stunned by some seedless juice?)"

"Okay Mr. Rowley," beamed Sarah.

("Okay indeed, you fruity little fucklette,") smiled Rowley silently.

7

"Why have you booked the drama hall for this lesson, Mr. Rowley?"

"Collision theory."

"Oh?" said Sarah, uncomprehendingly.

Rowley had twenty six eleven year olds positioned on the huge stage of the drama hall.

"For a chemical reaction to happen you need two things, activation energy leading to particles colliding. You are the particles, and as vibrant young Einstein's you have all the energy necessary!"

Sarah smiled at Rowley adoringly. Class 7F were then told to run around the stage at random. Occasionally they bumped into each other. The stage was then partitioned by chairs, to half its size.

"We have now increased the concentration of the particles, or, in the case of gases, increased the pressure. Now run!" More and more collisions!

"Get the idea?" asked Rowley.

"Yes sir!" said 7F, in unison.

For the last lesson of the day Rowley was back in his laboratory with the adoring Sarah watching, and taking notes. Twelve 17-year-old 6th formers had come to be entertained and educated.

Rowley would not let them down. First he checked what Miranda Thring was wearing.

("Yes, your little pink low cut number, you pubescent strumpet!" mused Rowley, "which lucky little pimple-squeezer is squeezing those Miranda?")

Rowley began.

"To explain variable valency of the Transition Elements one can liken some of the outer electrons to floating voters, changing their allegiance from one party to the next, and by so doing, also changing their colour."

Brilliant, and Miranda Thring had leaned forward exposing even more of her delicious cleavage, which suited Rowley just fine. He was off to 'The Spit and Sawdust' later.

Chapter 2

This unlikely quartet, were, arguably, the best fishing team in the NW of England. On Saturday they could prove it at St. Helens. The winning team would be automatic entrants into the 'big one'—The Irish Match! They had fished as a team for three seasons and, in the 30 matches they had contested they had won 22, been second 3 times, third twice and been unplaced only 3 times. This was a phenomenal track record and they were clear favourites for the match on Saturday. The venue was the huge 'Pitts Reservoir', St. Helens. It would depend on the draw. Low number pegs were preferable. There were 40 pegs on the reservoir and they knew how best to fish most of them. Tonight was a 'tactics' meeting in The Spit and Sawdust.

Dave Tonks always arrived early at the pub.

"Pinta Golden Dave?" asked Pam the barmaid.

"Yeah, ta."

And Pam duly mixed half of lager with half of bitter and handed the foaming brew to Dave.

"Big match on Saturday, Dave."

"Yeah, tough one too," moaned Dave.

"Favourites aren't ya?"

"Yeah, kissa death," moaned Dave again.

"Gerrawaywithya! Y'aven't lost a match in ages!"

"Yeah, that's the problem, could be our turn to blank."

"Cheerful sod aren't ya Dave?"

Dave shrugged his shoulders, lit up a Marlboro Light, pulled his copy of 'Improve Your Freshwater Fishing' out of his arse pocket, picked up his pint of golden, slurped off its head, and sauntered over to the reserved table in the far corner of the bar.

"Usual Rowley?" asked Pam.

"Indeed Pam, (and stir the cream on my pint with an erect left nipple please.)"

Pam set down Rowley's pint of Guinness and planted a huge pork pie next to it. Rowley's 'usual'.

Rowley was a fallen vegetarian. He had suffered Trish's nut salads, veggie burgers, and Soya-enhanced tasteless crap for over 15 years and had secretly been eating meat for the past 10! It coincided with having his balls deactivated. After the snip he had treated himself to a thick juicy 12 oz rump steak and hadn't looked back since. Trish didn't know, of course, which suited Rowley just fine.

Pam looked at Rowley's pie and a pint and commented.

"Tasty pair that."

Rowley smiled, scanned Pam's ample cleavage and thought,—'tasty indeed Pamela, a tasty pair indeed my love'.

"Salutations young David," said Rowley, arriving at the reserved table.

"'Lo Rowley. Alright mate?"

"Positively ebullient David, my boy!" enthused Rowley.

"Y'wha?" asked Dave.

The intellectual chasm between Rowley and Dave would take a starship traveling at warp speed 9, a thousand years to breach. Nonetheless, in a straight fishing match head to head on lake or river, Rowley knew he would come in second to Dave every time, and he respected him for that. Rowley decided to match Dave's mental capacity.

"Any good boils on the brew Dave?"

"Yeah! Clock this," and Dave smiled.

Dave rolled up the left leg of his faded denims to reveal a nurturing boilette erupting in its throbbing infancy from Dave's left knee.

"Could be a stonker that, Dave," enthused Rowley, ("you poor unfortunate infected Neolithic cretin.")

"What will it be tonight, Sid," asked Pam.

Sid Lennon changed his preferred drink as often as his underpants, at least once a week.

"Apart from you on toast Pam, I'll have to settle for a pint of lager love, oh, and a bag of pork scratchins."

"Fancy an Extra Strong Mint?" asked Pam, after smelling Sid's breath again.

"No ta love, spoil the taste of me pint."

Sid had tried in vain to pull the busty Pam for ages and he was sure she would crack one day. Jonah Carter had cracked it the first day he had met Pam and, right on cue, in strode the cocky cockney. Pam's flaps twitched in memory of a 9inch meat injection.

"The same?" enquired Pam. Carter always asked for the 'same'.

"Same it is Pam. You look sonnink stunnin' tonight gel, got a hot date?"

"Play your cards right," said Pam, with a twinkle in her eye. Jonah felt a twinkle in his underpants. Dirty Sid frowned.

"Hey up Jonah, how y'doin'?" asked Sid.

"Blindin' my son, had an absolute blindin' day. Fancy a Polo mint Sid?"

"No ta," said Sid. "What is it with these mints?" he thought, but couldn't fathom it.

"The other two here?" asked Jonah.

Sid nodded to the corner and Jonah smiled at the sight of Dave, his left trouser leg rolled up to the knee, with Rowley feigning interest in an exposed maturing boil. Dave and Rowley exchanged pleasantries with Sid and Jonah, and then quickly got down to business. Dave opened up a map of Pitts Reservoir, St. Helens and spread it out on the table. Pegs 1 to 40 were clearly marked and Dave had fished some of them last weekend.

"So Dave, whatcha fink son?" asked Jonah.

"It fished crap last Sunday. Five fuckin' hours and I only managed a 20lb bag, mainly roach and perch, few skimmers, one good tench."

"Whatcha reckon then, Dave?" asked Sid.

"Less than a 100lb team bag is gonna win this one. Depends on the pegs we draw, the big pike are feeding, really fuckin' up the silver fish."

"Any bream showing David?" enquired Rowley.

"Gone t'fuckin' sleep. Bit hit and miss."

"Come on then my son, what's the game plan?" asked Jonah.

Dave pointed to the map "Pegs 1 to 13, no problem. Gravel bottom, no weeds, and 6 to 9 feet deep. Tackle up 3 rods. Rod 1, match rod on the waggler. Fish 6inches over depth, size 20 hook. Start with double pinkie; move to single red maggot or caster. Loose feed maggots over a bed of hemp and caster with red ground bait. If you catch regular, stay with it, if not move on to the feeder. Rod 2, brown ground bait in the feeder, size 16 hook, single thin worm as hook bait. If it's really slow it's shit or bust. Rod 3, bait runner with heavy tackle, size 10 hook, trout-pellet paste as hook bait and pray for a big carp."

The other three team members simply nodded their approval.

"Lead on McDuff," instructed Rowley.

"Y'wha?" said Dave.

"Carry on David, (you blithering yet brilliant dunderhead)".

"Pegs 14 to 30, lorra Lilly pads. Same match rod as before but a heavier bottom and size 18 hook with caster and sweet corn hook bait. Some conkin' tench around the pads. If it's dead around the pads, then go on the feeder. If it's totally crap, and you have less than 20lb in your keep net, rod 3 will be a dead bait for pike."

Again the other three nodded their approval. Dave saw this as the sign to continue.

"Pegs 31 to 40, fuckin' naff. Lorra thick weed. Try floating caster to bring roach to the surface and catch them there. On a feeder use 4lb line straight through. Carp and Pike can completely fuck you up, so try to build up a bag of bits. That's it."

"Okay. Cheers Dave," said Sid, "the draw for the pegs is at 8am. 'All in' at 9am and all out at 2pm, it's a regular 5-hour match. Any fish over 3lb is to be individually weighed by a bailiff and put back in. If you're into a fish on the whistle, you have 10 minutes to land it or it won't count."

"Splendid Sidney, fancy a Trebor mint?" Sid nodded, no. "Now let me get you all a refill then," and Rowley beetled off to the bar to do the honours. Sid, Dave and Rowley, realizing the importance of the match were full of nervous energy and sipped their respective brews deep in thought. Jonah was upbeat.

"F'fack's sake lads, come on! We're the best, the fackin' dog's bollocks. There are only them tarts from 'The Ring-O-Bells' who can even push us close. Fack me! If Dave pulls one of the first 13 pegs we're home and dry!"

The quartet broke up early at 10pm. Dave and Sid shared a taxi home. Jonah and Rowley were within walking distance. Jonah slipped busty Pam his new mobile phone number, and, with a wink, hoped he might be slipping her considerably more later on. Jonah and Rowley walked and chatted together until their paths went different ways.

"Okay Rowley old son, see you Saturday at the Pitts," said Jonah, "be lucky!"

"Good night Jonah."

Rowley felt good until he envisaged his nut-cutlet supper and glass of insipid Bulgarian white wine.

This, coupled with the nightly report from 'mother earth' Trish on what his brood had been up to that day, bought him back to reality with a jolt. Economic constraints had kept all his kids at home. Three of them were at Liverpool University. Fleur, 22 still agonizing whether she was on a 'first' or a 2-1 in her final year B.A. History and Politics. Abigail, 20, in her second year of a B.Sc. in chemistry and flying. Dougal, 19, trying desperately not to fail his first year of Media Studies and then, there was Jake, 17, hacking his way through Double Maths and Physics 'A' level.

It was, however, the thought of the imminent supper, which nauseated Rowley. He took a short detour via the local Deli, and purchased the largest Frankfurter sausage on sale and consumed it with impish relish, which suited Rowley just fine.

Saturday morning 8.20am, Pitts Reservoir, St. Helens, and the draw was bad.

'Would you fackin' Adam and Eve it, not one peg lower than 20! Fack me, this is gonna be hard work!" moaned Jonah.

What made matters worse, was the fact that three of the tarts from The Ring-O-Bells had bagged pegs 2, 6, and 7!

"Come on lads! We can do this! Be positive. We have to go for it. Come on!" said Rowley, trying to sound upbeat but with his heart in his boots.

They trudged off to their pegs. Sid on 24, Jonah on 27, Rowley on 32 and Dave on 38. They were the best fishermen at the venue on, arguably, the worst pegs. Fucking Nora!

All contestants were tackled up by 8.55am. A whistle sounded followed by a shout of 'ALL IN' and the match was on. Sid and Jonah knew the onus was on them and their concentration was really focused. They cursed when they missed bites, but they missed precious few and caught steadily if unspectacularly. Sid did have one 'weigher' though, a 3lb 7oz tench, which would help.

Dave, as always, fished like a man possessed. He didn't miss a single bite but apart from a bream and a tench both over 2lbs he was amassing a bag of bits, small roach and perch mainly. This contest would be very close.

Rowley was having a nightmare. After four hours, he calculated he had netted less than 10lb of fish. He had been snapped four times and had missed umpteen bites. He felt sick and angry. Intermittently he would scan the three 'tarts' from the Ring-O-Bells through his binoculars on pegs 2, 6 and 7 and they each looked to be bagging up Rowley tasted defeat. He called Sid and Jonah on his mobile.

"Weight Sid?"

"Twenty, maybe twenty five pounds."

"Weight Jonah?"

"Over twenty."

Rowley knew that Dave would fish the peg from hell, number 38, better than anyone but dared not phone him. Dave's concentration was too intense.

"Oh fuck it all!" exclaimed Rowley on being snapped for the 5th time. He despairingly threw his match rod up the bank, tears of frustration and anger welling up in his eyes.

"I've fucking blown it!" he hissed. There were only six minutes to go.

He snatched up his carp rod, ripped off the bolt rig and attached a steel multi-hooked pike trace. He reached into his net, took out a small roach, clonked it to death, and fitted it to the trace. He cast some twenty yards to his left and bobbled the dead bait on the bottom near a reed bed.

"Clutching at fucking straws," said the bailiff standing behind him, "there's only a couple of minutes to go."

("Fuck off and drown yourself!") thought Rowley.

Just then, the water by the reed bed exploded and Rowley's 3lb test curve carp rod bent double.

"Lucky twat," said the eloquent bailiff, and shortly after that the whistle blew."You got ten minutes to land that pal, or it don't count," chuckled the bailiff, who then took his watch off to time Rowley.

"Jesus Christ it's a monster!" said Rowley, "and only ten minutes to land it!"

Rowley had 8lb line straight through. Normally he would run his quarry, wear it out and land it at his leisure. 'Don't bully your fish' was Rowley's favourite saying. 'It will slip the hook or break you if you bully it.' Another Rowleyism.

"Fuck off Rowley!" Rowley said to himself.

"Y'wha?" said the bailiff.

Rowley pulled the pike near to the surface to keep it out of the weeds, but it was still some fifteen yards away. It then started to tail-walk out of the water!

"Oh, fuck it all!" shouted Rowley.

"It'll break you," said the smiling, vindictive bailiff, "three minutes left!"

"Three minutes, is that all!" bawled Rowley.

"And twenty seven seconds," added the bailiff.

Beads of sweat pitted Rowley's brow. No time for niceties, this was shit or bust! Rowley pulled hard then dropped his rod and reeled in frantically. Pulled up, dropped down, reeled in. With each pull he waited for the line to snap. This was no way to treat a large predatory fish.

"Less than a minute," said the bailiff.

Rowley threw in his large carp landing net and let it sink in front of him. He played the huge pike over the net, and then, disaster! The line snapped and the pike shot deep into the water. Rowley howled in agony and then saw his landing net pole disappear under water. He grabbed the pole and could feel the power of the huge pike writhing. The pike had swum headlong into his landing net! Rowley swiftly dispensed with protocol. He jumped balls deep into his swim and hauled the landing net and the pike onto the bank, almost collapsing with the effort. Rowley looked up imploringly at the bailiff.

"You lucky twat, eight seconds left."

Rowley wept with relief.

"18lb 3oz. What a snorting fish. Well done lad!" and the bailiff added 18lb 3oz to the 9lb 7oz of tiddlers Rowley had netted.

Rowley eased the monster back into the water and kissed it on its flank.

"Esox Lucius, my precious," declared Rowley in his best Gollumesque.

"You're fucking nuts," said the bailiff.

"Quite so, quite so," said a delighted Rowley as Esox Lucius shot back into its hunting ground like a silver bolt.

The weigh-in would be close. The Ring-O-Bells had totaled 117lb 2oz. No other team was close. Sid, Jonah and Rowley had a combined weight of 86lb 9oz. They waited for Dave's weight. The bailiff read it out.

"Dave Tonks, 31lb 3oz."

Was it enough? Sid and Rowley just couldn't do the maths for love nor money. Jonah could.

"117lb 12oz, well fack me rigid! We've won by the weight of me todger! We done it, blindin'! We're off to Ireland for the big one lads!"

The 'Big One' was 'The All England Rod and Line Championship.' It was scheduled for the last week in May, usually a good month for fishing. The match was to be accumulative over five days at five different venues. Later that week, when the venues were announced, the team was ecstatic.

Chapter 3

Fergal O'Shaunessey had a flea named Colin. Colin had come to him one night, and took up residence.

After nine pints of Guinness and a monumental belt of the Blackbush, (in celebration of the betrothal of his gangling and demented nephew Sean, to the pneumatic Assumpta Monahan—who was already three months into a less than immaculate conception,) Fergal now lay prostrate and naked on his grubby single divan, snoring thunderously into the black night of a hot and humid August.

Fergal was awoken by a tickle in the vicinity of his belly button. He furrowed his brow, arched up his head and looked down his nostrils at the flea.

"Well, will ya look at that?" he said giggling.

"Have ya got a name at all little fella?" he enquired of the bug. The flea said nothing.

"Cat got ya tongue, has it? Well, 'tis right and proper that all God's creatures have a name. Do ya not agree?"

Had Fergal stumbled across a deaf flea? Maybe it was mute.

"Well . . . let me see now," and Fergal stroked his bristled chin and pulled on his lower lip, deep in thought. He then announced, "You are now Colin . . . Colin the flea. What do ya think?"

Colin must have been deep in thought too. He said nothing.

"And what type of flea are ya Colin, a nit or a crab?" asked Fergal, "well let's find out now," and Fergal jiggled the blubber on his belly to make the flea move.

"If it's to the North y'll be movin' Colin, then it is a nit-type flea you are. To the South . . . a crab!" proclaimed Fergal. Colin moved north.

"'Tis a nit you are!" said Fergal.

However, after a few centimetres, and to Fergal's amazement, Colin changed tack and headed northwest and, on reaching Fergal's right armpit, duly took up residence.

"'Tis unique you are Colin," Fergal whispered into his armpit and started to chuckle, then fart, and finally snore his way back to unconsciousness.

Colin was a thoughtful resident. He only fed when Fergal was asleep and, when he felt like a less sweaty diet; he would embark on the occasional nocturnal sortie to Fergal's right eye brow.

Although Fergal was a good Catholic, who regularly gassed Farther McCartney through the grille of the confessional with breath laced with halitosis, nicotine and remorse, Fergal vowed not to kill Colin.

"There might be something in this reincarnation," he mused, "what if Colin was me dear old Mammy come back to me. Holy Jesus now there's a thought! And I've only gone and given her a man's name! Oh, bugger it all!"

Fergal O'Shaunessy had an intellect slightly less than Colin's. As a child he had lost the little toe on his left foot to the frostbite and could therefore only count to nineteen with any certainty. Notwithstanding this limited mental capacity, Fergal O'Shaunessy had been born with the brilliant hands. He could not only design the most intricate patterns for silk-screens, but he could also copy any pattern onto copper metal and mild steel. Fergal's masterpiece was to be the 20 Punt note. His templates to produce perfect copies of the note would be breathless in their accuracy. All it needed was the correct paper and inks. Brendan McHugh would be the paper and inks man. Fergal and Brendan would come together as the result of a prophetic accident.

"Fergal, can y' make me something in the metal for me mate Brendan?" asked Mick Kelly.

"I can," said Fergal.

"How about dis, den?" and Mick pulled out a 10 pound sterling note with a photograph covering the Queen's face.

"The Queen of England looks like a fella," said Fergal.

"It is," said Mick, "It's me mate, Brendan."

"Oh," replied Fergal.

"'Tis for a present y' see," said Mick.

"No, I don't see," said Fergal.

"I'll explain," said Mick.

"Get me a pint first," said Fergal.

"I will," said Mick.

Brendan McHugh had worked as a print master at The Royal Mint in London for twelve years. He was brilliant with the inks, which produced the multifarious colors on the bank notes of several different countries. However, the gambling bug bit Brendan. A small each way winning bet on a horse developed into a disease. The horses, dogs, football pools, the lottery, poker, brag, roulette, Brendan would bet on anything. He even joined an Internet casino.

His mounting debts made him a desperate man. Brendan was headhunted by Albert Onions, a convicted counterfeiter from the East End of London. Albert was good, not brilliant, and had designed several passable templates for the £50 sterling note. Albert was also under surveillance by The Metropolitan Police Fraud Squad.

Brendan and Albert built a machine capable of producing £50 notes. The frame of the machine, it's electronics, the device for producing different serial numbers, the correct paper and inks, were Brendan's input. Six 50-pound note templates were Albert's.

Brendan was meticulous about security. He always assumed, quite rightly as it turned out, that he and Albert were under scrutiny by the police. When he and Albert decided to go into production they knew they had to disappear and not divulge the whereabouts of their moneymaking machine. They started early. Independently they would use the London Underground for hours, hopping on the tube and alighting at different stations. They would then hop from taxi to taxi before going back onto the tube. They would eventually meet up in a disused Victorian sewer, which lead to the river Thames just west of Putney. Always at night, at a pre-arranged time, they would surface from the sewer and hop onto a barge piloted by two of their associates. They hopped off under a bridge while the barge continued down the Thames. They would then wait for a minimum of an hour and, in the dead of night, walk to a lock-up garage near Putney where the 'machine' was housed.

The police never did locate the machine and for D.I. Steve Kendall it became his Holy Grail. Albert and Brendan were eventually arrested for passing counterfeit £50 notes and were banged up in Wormwood Scrubs for six years apiece. Out in four.

Mick Kelly was there to meet Brendan on his release. They embraced, backslapped, laughed, and hopped a cab to the nearest Irish bar to drink the Guinness. Brendan and Mick were old mates who grew up together in the back streets of Sligo. They chatted happily and reminisced the old days and after four pints of the black stuff, Mick finally declared, "I have a present for ya," and he handed his friend a £10 sterling note with the Queen's face supplanted with Brendan's. The note was printed in black and white on poor quality paper.

"Well, if they put you in prison for using the Queen of England's money, I thought y' should use your own!" and Mick and Brendan laughed heartily. Brendan then looked closely at the note.

"Jesus, Mary and Joseph," exclaimed Brendan, "this is feckin' brilliant!"

"'Tis only a joke," said Mick.

"No, Mick, the detail, I mean I've never seen anything as good as this! Who on earth put it together?"

"Fergal O'Shaunessey," said Mick, "he's always had the brilliant hands. Other than that, the man's a feckin' loony. I mean, he talks to his armpit!"

"What?" asked Brendan.

"Oh, never mind. Come on, lets hit the Jameson's," said Mick.

"I've got to meet this fella," said Brendan, "he has the gift in his hands."

"'Tis for sure," said Mick, "but there's only a couple of mothballs rolling around inside his skull."

"Never mind," said Brendan, "they say that genius and insanity are closely linked."

"'Tis true," said Mick, "Fergal is the thickest genius I know."

Brendan gave Mick the keys to the lock-up in Putney.

"Go back to Ireland," said Brendan, "wait a month, then come back, crate the machine, and have it transported to me Mammy's house in Sligo."

"I will," said Mick. And he did.

Martha D'Arcy was mildly insane. She was also a very wealthy woman. She had been born into an upper-crust English family in Gloucestershire some 45 years ago. Her upbringing was classical. Kindergarten, boarding school, and, in deference to her lineage,

Trinity College, Dublin and a double first in Philosophy, Politics and Economics. Her ancestors were the infamous D'Arcy's of County Wexford who had fled the old country at the height of the potato famine and settled in England, even though they still had a huge estate in Ireland, and owned almost half of the county.

Martha's outdoor pursuits, quite rightly included, shooting, fishing and hunting and she excelled at them all. At the age of 22, and still a virgin, she had become engaged to the master of the Gloucestershire Hunt, Major Ridley Palmer-Davidson. Ridley had finally won her heart by sharing a stirrup cup of scotch and Drambuie and singing the song 'Martha my Dear' by Paul McCartney, (even though it is about a dog.) On the day of their engagement, the galloping major, during a hunt, had fallen when his horse vaulted a high hedgerow, broken his neck and promptly died. He was 36.

His funeral was colorful. The pallbearers wore full hunting regalia of black riding hats, redcoats and jodhpurs and, to the sound of hunting horns, Ridley was interred together with the brush of the fox he had been hunting on that fateful day.

Martha was inconsolable. Hunting had taken away the man she had worshipped. She bristled with inner anger and rebelled against her lifestyle, particularly hunting, which she grew to loathe. Martha became a convert. She joined an organization to ban all forms of hunting, but after a few years of fruitlessly holding peaceful protests, she formed a radical, more proactive action group. Her parents ostracized their only child and, from being independently well off; Martha became extremely wealthy when her parents were killed in an air crash.

Her father was piloting his private Cessna Turboprop with his wife and four other friends on an excursion to the Scottish highlands for a fly-fishing weekend when his rudder fell off. With the loss of this aerodynamically vital component, gravity did the rest. The light aircraft plunged into the side of a Scottish mountain killing everyone on board.

Shooting, hunting and fishing, Martha hated them all. At the age of 30 she formed ASHAFA:—the Anti-Shooting-Hunting and Fishing-Association, which became the most radical and violent anti-blood sports association in Britain. It was also a monumental pain in the arse to the British police force for twelve years. The crunch came at a Gloucestershire Hunt one April. Martha had clearly become partially demented.

In her arsenal that day, Martha and her colleagues had, gas masks, whips, spiked baseball bats, pepper sprays, stun grenades and pipe-rockets. The dogs and horses were not direct targets; only the human animals were to be attacked. There would be mayhem!

The Gloucestershire Hunt assembled in the village of Lower Piddlington. It met outside, of course, 'The Fox and Hounds' pub. In the pub car park was a Ford Transit van, full of ASHAFA nutters. In another Ford Transit, a mile down the lane, sat the head nutter herself, Martha D'Arcy. Her van had a sliding roof, out of which jutted six curious metal tubes, which looked like sawn-off organ pipes.

The master of the hunt gave the signal for the car park ASHAFA recruits, unwittingly, as he sounded his horn to signify the start of the hunt. The sliding door of the van was flung back, and out leapt 10 ASHAFA soldiers in full battle fatigues, boots and gas masks. Three rapid pistol shots in the air, and the hounds were off! A stun grenade disorientated the horses, and the riders grappled with their reins as their steeds whinnied and reared up in panic. The ASHAFA team went to work with spiked baseball bats, driven into calves, knees, thighs and buttocks of the riders, who were also intermittently squirted with pepper spray. Several riders escaped and took off at frightening speed, leaping the hedgerow and galloping across open country. That's where Martha came in.

Her pipe-rockets were aimed 25 yards in front of the escaping horse riders. They were jettisoned, with incredible accuracy, in two banks of three through the roof of the van. On impact, in front of the terrified posse, the horses came to a shuddering halt, and inertia did the rest. Nine of the eleven riders were flung headlong from their steeds. One huntsman was dragged along unceremoniously with a boot caught in a stirrup, and, as this particular horse vaulted a low hedge, its passenger was duly deposited into the middle of it. One bewildered and terrified horsewoman clinging desperately to the neck of her horse escaped unscathed. Martha grinned gratuitously. This had been a good one indeed.

Martha stood bolt upright in the dock at the Old Bailey. England's premier criminal court had been especially chosen to emphasize the gravity of such violent, anti-establishment behavior. The judge, after all, was a senior member of the Leicestershire Hunt, and this case would give him inestimable pleasure! He turned to Martha to pronounce his judgment. Martha's piercing ice blue eyes stared unwaveringly ahead. She was dressed in her battle fatigues and a long black trench coat. Her exquisite, classical features were further accentuated by her trademark hairstyle. Her greying, auburn hair was swept back stringently into a round bun at the back of her head and was spiked diagonally with two large pins. She folded her arms and flared her nostrils. Her supporters in the public gallery looked on in awe.

"Martha Abigail Delilah D'Arcy, you have been found guilty of leading an organization responsible for heinous and violent crimes against society. For the past 12 years, your increasingly brutal methods of protest have culminated in the crime for which I now prepare to pass sentence. Your organization," he read through half-rimmed spectacles from a paper in front of him, "the, er, Anti-Shooting-Hunting and Fishing Association, ASHAFA for short is, from this day, outlawed. It will be disbanded and it's assets confiscated. It is by God's good grace that you and your associates do not stand here indicted for murder or manslaughter. You are a menace to society, and must be removed from it. Do you have anything to say before I pass sentence?"

"I do," she said.

"Go on," said the judge, with a nod of his head.

"We are unmoved and steadfast in our resolve. We will not be broken!" exclaimed Martha, as cheers rose from the public gallery. Eventually the court was called to order.

When the court was silent, the judge removed his spectacles and looking menacingly down at Martha D'Arcy pronounced, "You shall go to prison for five years."

As Martha was lead from the dock, she turned to the public gallery, gave a clenched fist salute with her right hand and a wicked wink with her left eye. Cheers and applause rang in her ears as she was removed from the court.

At Holloway Prison, Martha was a model inmate. She obeyed all the regulations, and for recreation, she read avidly and painted in watercolors. She also planned the next phase of her life. She would retire to her estate in County Wexford, Ireland and plot her revenge. Martha served three years and three months and was released. During this time her organization had been broken up, and some of her more fanatical followers had also had to serve custodial sentences. She needed time to reflect.

From the stern of the Super Seacat Ferry, she watched the famous Liver Birds of Liverpool dissolve into the Mersey, and, four hours later, she disembarked in Dublin. A further two hours on and Martha sat in a winged armchair in front of a roaring peat and coal fire in her family mansion at D'Arcyfields, Co. Wexford. She swirled a large brandy glass in her hands and drank from it, deep in thought. She despised the English. She despised all things

English. She was back home now, back to her ancestral roots, back in Ireland.

"He's fucking well up to something," said Detective Inspector Steve Kendall, Metropolitan Police, Fraud Squad, as he peered through field binoculars from the rear window of an unmarked VW Caravanette, parked 100 metres from Donna McHugh's cottage on the outskirts of Sligo.

"Yeah, and we're fucking well up shit creek without a fucking paddle!" said sergeant John Broadbent, Metropolitan Police, Fraud Squad, "right out of our jurisdiction, no right of arrest, nowt! Christ, how did I let you talk me into this? I could be lying on a beach in Benidorm. We're on holiday Steve, we're not working for the old bill!"

"I know John, I know. We can't involve the Micks just yet, you know that."

"Yeah, but its on their patch, the Garda have a right to know."

"We're tourists on a mission John. This is a private investigation. We'll pull in the Garda and clue them up when we get some hard evidence, and we are certain we can nail him."

Right on cue, Brendan McHugh marched out of the front door of his Mammy's house, jumped into his brand new Opel Astra, and drove off to meet Fergal O'Shaunessy.

"She's fecking well up to something," said Inspector Kieran O'Brien, Wexford County Garda, as he peered through field binoculars from the rear window of an unmarked Mercedes Benz Sprinter van 100 metres from Martha D'Arcy's mansion.

"How the feck can y' see anything from this far away?" asked P.C. Patrick Kelsey, Wexford County Garda.

"I've a good imagination," said Inspector O'Brien wryly.

"Spyin' on a mad Englishwoman seems barmy to me," said Paddy, "even her fecking name,—Martha Abigail Delilah D'Arcy spells MADD."

"That's two 'D's y' have there Paddy," said Kieran.

"What y' talking about?" asked Paddy.

"Forget it," said Kieran.

"Forget what?" asked Paddy.

Just then, Martha D'Arcy opened a side door of her mansion to four shady looking characters in anoraks.

Chapter 4

The Team received notification of the venues for 'The Irish Match'.

"Absolutely blindin'!" exclaimed Jonah. "It's on our manor lads, clock this!"

The venue statement read:—

> Day 1. LochAllen, Drumshambo.
>
> Day 2. RiverShannon, Jamestown
>
> Day 3. Loch Ree, Ballykeeran.
>
> Day 4. River Boyle, Battlebridge
>
> Day 5. LochDerg, Mountshannon

> First Prize:—100,000 Euros. No other prizes.

The team had regularly fished in this region of Ireland for the past four years and, this was, as Jonah put it, 'their manor'. They had knowledge of, and had fished all the venues listed successfully before.

"If we don't win this we should be disemboweled and de-scrotumised," said Rowley.

"Y'wha?" said Dave.

"Booked the digs, then Jonah?" asked Sid.

"Yeah, no probs," said Jonah, "it's 'The Shoal of Bream Lodge,' at Jamestown. Been there before. You'll find the landlady most accommodating!"

"How's that then, Jonah? "Asked Sid, "did you give her one?"

"Tried to my son, tried real hard," said Jonah.

"But she wouldn't let ya get your leg over?" enquired Sid.

"Not at all," said Jonah, "slippin' it in the old flaps was the easy part, just couldn't satisfy her. I gave up in the end. Which, I have to say, was a severe blow to my sexual pride."

"Great," enthused Sid, "I'll give her a right seeing to you!"

"You would be most welcome, my son, believe me. Fancy a Clarnico mint Sid?" said Jonah.

"No ta," said Sid, "what's the landlady's name?"

"The glorious Bernadette Clancy," replied Jonah, "she's some woman, Sid."

Bernadette Clancy had, for the past 17 years, been at 'the edge'. It was a source of continual regret that she had never passed beyond 'the edge', and experienced a full-blown orgasm.

At the age of 18, Bernadette Clancy, as virtuous and virginal as the driven snow itself, became Mrs. Bernadette McGuire. On this, her first wedding night, she was a picture of pubescent desire. She was tall at 5'9", and had a voluptuous untouched body. The beauty of her blonde hair, rounded cherubic face, and claret coloured lips, perfectly matched her rounded cherubic bosom, with their claret coloured areolae, and nipples the size of Brazil nuts. She had wide hips even then.

"Sure and she'll be having a large brood of healthy children," predicted her mother-in-law, the redoubtable Mary-Ann McGuire, as she looked at Bernadette's hips. Nobody was to know, including Bernadette herself that this stunning young colleen was, in fact, as sterile as a mule. Slung due south of these hips was an ample arse, which was destined to assume fearful proportions in later years.

The bridegroom, Micky McGuire, was a vibrant, strapping youth of 20 when he acquired the conjugal rights to Bernadette's bed. At the age of 29, he had finally acquired an everlasting erection, as he lay stiff with the rigor mortis in his imitation-silk lined coffin at his own wake. A massive heart attack had seen Micky pass over, spent and unfulfilled.

Micky McGuire had been fit, and the youngest ever captain of the local county Gaelic football team. His charming manner, his shock of wild ginger hair, his beautiful singing voice and his athletic 6'2" frame had made every young girl in the village wet and expectant with the dream of becoming his wife. However, it was big Bernadette who had won his heart, which was to burst 9 years later in the drunken effort to satisfy her.

Bernadette was always at 'the edge'. She almost had the biggest orgasm in all of Ireland, but never did. Oh, the sex was pleasurable to be sure, but she could never reach the summit.

"Go on, go on, oh go on!" she would implore as Micky did his best.

"Oh, 'tis lovely Micky, go on, go on go on!" she would gasp.

After almost two solid hours of taking her in reverse, holding her shoulders, and riding her at full throttle, Micky would beseech, "Jesus woman, have y' not come yet!"

"In a while . . . go on go on, I'm almost there!" begged his breathless wife.

Bernadette never arrived.

Sex was always the same for the McGuire's, and if nothing else, it kept Micky super-fit. However, as the years passed, Micky lost his happy-go-lucky nature and started to look like a defeated man. The straw which broke this camel's back, or more precisely, a heart valve, was the snide comments ascribed to his manhood.

"You've a dick the size of a horse, a body like Adonis himself, a magnificent woman, and not a single wee child to show for it in 9 years. Is them balls of yours full of tater-water, or what!" said Dermot McCourt, Micky's boss, after one too many pints.

"Would y' be after wantin' me to slip one in for ya? Hee, hee, hee" Dermot had giggled through nicotine yellow teeth, which were swiftly dispatched to the back of his throat by a crushing right hook from Micky, who, just as quickly, found himself unemployed.

Micky went on a bender. Later that night, fortified by a whole bottle of Bushmill's whiskey, he pumped the conjugal beejayzus out of his missus.

"Go on, go on, go on!"

After 10 minutes, a valve in his heart ruptured, and Micky had arrived in the afterlife. Bernadette hadn't arrived at all!

"Don't stop Micky! Go on, go on, oh go on!"

It became common knowledge that Micky had died on the job. People began looking at Bernadette through squinted eyes. She had loved Micky deeply and kept herself swathed in black for fully two years after his wake. She never went near another man and never touched herself, you know, down there at all, oh no. The desire inevitably returned and Bernadette turned to self-stimulation, which was mildly gratifying, but not as good as the real thing, or her craving to pass over the 'edge'. She sat, head bowed and ashamed in the confessional.

"Forgive me father it has been five weeks since my last confession."

"What is it my child?" asked Father McCartney.

"'Tis the desire for, for the excitement Father."

"The excitement?" enquired the priest.

"You know," started Bernadette, and then to herself, "well I suppose you don't know father."

"Know what?" asked the priest.

"Father, my husband died two years ago."

I know my child."

"Well, I've been good you know, not even sat in the company of a man all this time, but, but," and Bernadette started sobbing.

"There, there, my child, go on." said the priest, who was becoming uncomfortably aware of a stirring under his cassock.

"I've been playing with meself!" blurted Bernadette.

"Talk about it," said Fr. McCartney, now acutely embarrassed at spawning an erection.

"Well first it was the spin dryer."

"The spin dryer!" exclaimed the priest, and on calming down a little, "go on my child."

"It vibrates, and if you sit on it on full spin, well . . ."

"I see, I see," said Fr. McCartney, now covering his eyes with his right hand, trying desperately to quell his own arousal.

"Then it was me knickers," said Bernadette.

"Oh, good God," thought the priest, "your knickers?"

"Well, yes, I've been rubbin' meself down there, with me knickers, while I'm wearing them."

"And?" enquired a breathless Fr. McCartney.

"Then I got me a penny candle," sobbed Bernadette.

That was it! The confession was over as far as the priest was concerned.

"That's enough, my child, quite enough," he gasped, "say five Hail Mary's and four Our Father's, and please don't come back for a while!"

With that, father McCartney slammed shut the grille of the confessional, bit his lower lip in disgust at his own biology and rustled off to the lavatory. As his seed hit the porcelain he offered the same advice he had given to Bernadette in absolution of himself.

Bernadette was confused. She hadn't even made a full confession. She supposed that the large banana, and the 'Orgasmo deluxe', purchased under plain brown paper cover from 'Dinosaur Dildos, Dublin' would have to wait until next time.

At the age of 28, a widow is fair game in a small village and a few men had shared Bernadette's bed over the next four years. Only the married men left thanking the Almighty that their wives were not of the same sexual disposition as Bernadette.

"Go on, go on, go on, indeed," had said one exhausted punter, "me dick's still sore!"

Down at the confessional, Father McCartney was going grey.

After a brief courtship, Bernadette McGuire, nee Clancy, became Mrs. Bernadette O'Hara. Tommy O'Hara, a widower of 52, was a good man. He was a farmer with several cows and horses and a smallholding of some thirty acres. Although he was 22 years older than his wife, he was still young at heart. Two years later, and still 22 years older than his wife, he died of a stroke, and yes, like Micky McGuire, he was on the job too.

Bernadette sold the farm, and had a guesthouse built. It was called 'The Shoal of Bream Lodge, Shannonside". In her mid thirties and twice widowed, ultimate sexual gratification had never come, and, being infertile; she had no children to cosset. The nubile Bernadette let herself go somewhat. The ample bosom now assumed melonesque proportions, as had her huge arse. Her days on the spin dryer dried up, as did the use of her other mechanical sexual aids. Father McCartney thanked God.

Bernadette assumed her maiden name, and busied herself, as a good Irish European. She served her guests wholesome Irish fare, and provided them with a drying room, an outhouse full of shelves for their fishing tackle, and refrigerators for their bait. Bernadette's main customers were English fishermen. She looked at the booking reference for Jonah Carter and his three colleagues, and felt a twinge of arousal.

"Now that boy had come real close," she said to herself, and smiled at the memory.

Chapter 5

Brendan McHugh arrived at Donna's Bar in Rooskey County Leitrim, and ordered a pint of Guinness. He looked around the bar, sipping his pint, and quickly ascertained that the man in the far corner, sitting alone, and talking to his right armpit was the man with the brilliant hands, Fergal O'Shaunessy. He walked over to Fergal, who quickly ended his one-sided conversation with Colin the flea, and spoke.

"Is it Fergal O'Shaunessy I'm talking to?" he said.

"It is," replied Fergal.

"Pleased to meet you," said Brendan, who held out his hand for Fergal to shake. Brendan sat down, took from his pocket the 10-pound sterling note with his face on it, and spread it out on the table.

"'Tis yourself that made this, am I right?"

"You're right," replied Fergal.

"It's brilliant," said Brendan, "you certainly have the gift in them hands Fergal."

"I do," said Fergal, matter-of-factly.

"How would you like to make yourself a whole pile of money?" asked Brendan.

"I would like that," said Fergal, a man of few words.

"It's illegal," warned Brendan.

"I care not," said Fergal.

Brendan took out from his wallet a 20 punt note and spread it out in front of Fergal.

"Could you copy this, leaving out the serial numbers?" asked Brendan.

"I could," was the reply.

"Could you do 10 exact copies in the metal?" asked Brendan.

"Yes, now where is all this leading to?" asked Fergal.

Brendan told him about his plan.

By the end of that May, all old Irish currency was to be completely replaced by Euros. All old banknotes had to be encashed for Euros by May 31st., after which they would become valueless. Brendan's plan was, with the help of Fergal's brilliant hands, to make the equivalent of two million counterfeit Irish punts, which they would periodically change, up to the deadline date, for genuine Euros. The beauty of this endeavor was simple. Irish punts exchanged for Euros were sprayed with pink dye, so they could not be used as valid currency, and then sent to Dublin for incineration on the same day. Evidence of their criminal activity went up in smoke on the day of each exchange.

Brendan told Fergal of his 'machine', which could hold 10 templates. The correct inks and paper would be used as well as the device to change the serial numbers on each note. Brendan also told of his methods of 'ageing' most of the punts produced so that they looked well used. Brendan and his team would start in Sligo, periodically visiting every bank, and exchanging several thousand of the counterfeit punts for real Euros.

They would then move by motor launch along the length of the River Shannon and it's associated lochs, from Sligo to Limerick. They would stop off along the way to visit local banks and exchange their punts for Euros. They would finally meet up in Limerick where the last punt for Euro exchange would take place and the team would then divide up the spoils. Brendan was acutely aware of random Garda checkpoints on the roads. He had therefore decided to keep the counterfeit notes, and newly exchanged Euros, in large plastic color-coded bags on a motor launch instead of in a car or a van.

"'Tis a marvelous idea," said Fergal.

"So what do you think?" asked Brendan.

"I think I'd like another pint," said Fergal, and after drinking it enquired of Brendan, "and what would be in it for me?"

"The Euro equivalent of a quarter of a million Irish punts," said Brendan.

"Sounds fair to me," said Fergal.

"How long would it take you to produce the 10 templates?" asked Brendan.

"Five days," said Fergal confidently.

"You're on," said Brendan, and the two men shook hands.

"In five days my man, Dermot Goodchild, will contact you. He will pick up the templates and give you a down payment of 25,000 Euros. Is that okay?" asked Brendan.

"It all sounds fine to me," said Fergal.

D.I. Steve Kendall and Sergeant John Broadbent sat in the opposite corner of Donna's bar to Fergal and Brendan, looking, for all the world, like two gay English tourists.

"Did you see him lay those notes on the table John?" asked Steve.

"He's back in business all right," said John.

Brendan McHugh said goodbye to Fergal O'Shaunessy and shook one of his brilliant hands again. D.I. Steve Kendall and Sgt. John Broadbent decided to follow Fergal and try to find out exactly what he was up to. Fergal sat for a while smiling to himself. He then clapped his hands together gleefully and announced to his right armpit, "Did ya hear that Colin?" he enquired of the flea, "thousands of Euros! We'll be rich!"

Kendall and Broadbent looked at each other in disbelief.

"He's a fucking nutter," said Broadbent.

"You said it," said Kendall.

As soon as Fergal had cranked into life his ancient Ford Escort and moved off, Kendall and Broadbent followed in their equally ropy VW Caravanette.

Martha D'Arcy led four of her new associates into her private study of D'Arcyfields House. They all sat down around a large polished oak table, which shimmered in the glow from the peat and coal open-hearth fire. Martha walked towards her drinks cabinet and, pointing, enquired, "What would you like to drink?"

All four colleagues, two women and two men requested the same drink, Jameson's whiskey, with no ice.

After two years in Ireland, Martha D'Arcy was beginning to become the proactive anarchist again. There was no ritualized hunting as in England, and precious little shooting to demonstrate against. However, one of Ireland's biggest tourist industries had recently been given a massive shot in the arm from Europe. English anglers were pouring back into Ireland in droves. They were coming to reacquaint themselves with the glorious rivers Shannon, Boyle and Erne, and the wonderful lochs. Their saviour had been the great 'European Commission'!

On joining the European Union, the Commission was appalled at the third-world economic status of The Emerald Isle, and subsequently pumped in billions of Euros to secure Ireland's renaissance.

The major reason for the decline, particularly in course fishing, was the increasing inaccessibility of the rivers and lochs to anglers. Through under-funding riverbanks had become overgrown and unkempt. On the borders of the lochs grew banks of reeds.

38

Fishermen had to wear chest—waders and stand in four and a half feet of water in order to cast beyond the reeds, and be able to hook and play fish successfully. This was not the most pleasurable way to fish, all day, every day, on a fishing holiday. English anglers had been defecting to Denmark Holland and France.

The European Commission, realizing that one of Ireland's biggest economic assets was falling into disrepair, moved in with its huge monetary muscle. The riverbanks were made accessible, and areas were cut into these riverbanks where anglers could sit and fish in comfort. Overhanging tree branches were cut away to give anglers an easier cast into the rivers, and tonnes of riverweed and lily pads were dredged from the riverbeds to reduce the snags encountered by anglers when they had hooked a fish.

The lochs were absolutely transformed. Huge wooden walkways and platforms were built well beyond the reaches of the border reeds. Anglers could easily trundle all their gear onto these excellent platforms and fish with consummate ease. Indeed, many of the new platforms were specifically designed to accommodate disabled anglers. At every loch there were huge informative placards announcing:—(i) The name of the loch (ii) The species of fish that could be caught (iii) The rules and regulations governing fishing the loch, and (iv) The fact that the improvements to the loch had been brought about by 95% funding by the EU and 5% by the Irish Government.

Angling in Ireland was definitely back on the agenda for thousands of English fishermen. For the first time in 8 years, The All England Rod and Line Championship was being held back in Ireland. This important annual event carried tremendous kudos, and the Irish were pleased to be the hosts again.

Martha D'Arcy didn't like this one iota. The thought of the English, traipsing around Ireland catching, maiming and killing Irish fish was not to be tolerated. Martha had long since disowned her English heritage and had reverted back to her ancestral Irish roots. She had founded FOIF, the Friends Of Irish Fish. She had also had published and distributed every dubious 'fact' regarding the pain thresholds of fish, and how inhumane and cruel fishing was. Her protests to date had been well organized and, although sometimes rowdy, they were, for the most part, peaceful. Now was the time to flex the association's muscles and become violently proactive. Her plan was to unceremoniously terminate the last fishing match of The All England Rod and Line Championships on the lower reaches of Loch Derg at the end of May.

Her four most senior officers were now in attendance at D'Arcyfields house to go over the finer details of her plan. She unfolded a huge map of the southern tip of Loch Derg, the lower reaches.

"The English anglers will be positioned on these wooden platforms, numbers 1 through to 36. This final match is scheduled for five hours, between 0900 and 1400. I shall move in at precisely 1300. This is a major English sporting event; there are over 4 million English anglers, many of whom like to be updated on the progress of their favourite regional team. There will, therefore, be huge media cover for the last match so we are assured of maximum exposure for our efforts." Martha and her four most senior soldiers then went on to detail FOIF's strategy for the day.

Inspector Kieran O'Brien peered through the night sights of his field binoculars at the four shadows now leaving D'Arcyfields House. It was amazing how, in pitch darkness, he could make out the features of all five phantoms in an iridescent green light. He adjusted the electronic zoom focusing and trained his binoculars on the one person with his anorak hood down.

"Feck me, if it isn't Kathleen Connolly!" he said.

"And whose Kathleen Connolly?" asked P.C. Patrick Kelsey.

"Couple of years ago she did three months for the possession."

"For the possession of what?" asked Patrick.

"Semtex," informed Kieran.

"What's Semtex?" asked Patrick.

"For feck's sake Paddy! It's the plastic explosive!"

"Feck me," said Paddy, "this is getting serious."

And it was.

Chapter 6

The Spit and Sawdust's official championship team name was NorthWest One. On all correspondence however, Rowley, Jonah, Dave and Sid were simply referred to as NW(i). For, what every one referred to as, 'The Irish Match', there were nine teams in total, which included 34 men and 2 women, from all over England. The other teams were:—

> North One, N(i)
> NorthEast One, NE(i)
> Midlands One, MID(i)
> Midlands Two, MID(ii)
> SouthWest One, SW(i)
> SouthEast One. SE(i)
> SouthEast Two, SE(ii) and,
> South One, S(i)

The boys from The Spit and Sawdust, NW(i), knew some of the other anglers, but by no means all of them. Dave Tonks had, however, taken the time to read about all the other teams and how they had qualified for the Final Championship. Dave had already sussed out the most powerful opposition.

And so it transpired, that on the night before they sailed off to Ireland, the Fab Four, or NW(i) were downing a few pints at their local, and talking tactics, tackle and bait ad nauseam. They were each of them, extremely good all round anglers, with Dave being the best. Nonetheless, each of the others had specific strengths too.

'Dirty' Sid Lennon got the best out of canals and rivers. As a lad, when the River Mersey was little more than an open sewer, Sid had acquired this ability to 'read' the river and, invariably, would know where to catch fish. He would catch whilst others struggled.

Sid would, therefore, be an invaluable asset to have on the River Shannon and River Boyle.

Rowley very, very rarely lost a big fish. If any of them was to hook a large Carp, Barbel or Pike, Rowley would be odds-on the best bet to successfully land it.

Jonah's claim to fame was bagging-up on bream. He loved it.

"Better than sex, catching slabs of snot!" he would enthuse.

In a match, Jonah would carefully bait up a specific area of his swim, and then fish elsewhere for an hour or so! He had this uncanny sixth sense as to when the bream would move into his pre-baited swim. When he was on a roll, hooking and landing bream, he would sing;

> "Bream lover where are you . . ." or
> "All I have to do is Bream, Bream, Bream . . ." or
> "Breams are made of this . . ." or
> "Have you ever seen a Bream walking, well I have."

When Jonah was in full endless chorus, his mates knew he was on his way to a 100lb bag of bream. The end of May would see the shoals of bream moving from the rivers to the lochs in Ireland. Jonah could be in his element.

The five matches in The All England Rod and Line Championship were to be held from the Monday to the Friday of the last week in May. The team had decided to travel to Ireland on the Saturday before. This would give them ample time to settle into their digs and order sufficient bait from Kelly the Kraut.

Sunday would be used to reccy the five venues and possibly pick up any local inside knowledge.

"Fancy a peppermint chewy, Sid?" said Dave, offering Sid Lennon a stick of chewing gum.

"No, ta," said Sid. "Right lads, we're booked on The Super Seacat, Liverpool to Dublin, 8am in the morning."

"Managed to get an upgrade, Sid?" asked Rowley.

"Too fuckin' true mate! No second class travel for Team NW(i)!" proclaimed Sid, and his mates laughed and nodded in agreement.

"So what's the opposition lookin' like then, Dave?" asked Jonah.

"Bloody good, all of 'em," said Dave, "but we're up there with the best of 'em. The teams to keep an eye on are Midlands One, and SouthEast Two. Both these teams have got some real form, and will give us a run for our money.

"Who are these slags anyhow?" asked Jonah, "you got the team lists haven't you Dave?"

"Yeah, I sent off for them specially," said Dave, "not many others bother."

Dave reached into the arse pocket of his denims and pulled out the team lists.

"Here we are," he said, "and the second team listed is NW(i), none other than: (a) D.M. Tonks, (b) J.A. Carter, (c) J.P. Rowley and (d) S. Lennon."

"What does the 'M' stand for, Dave?" asked Rowley.

"Melvyn," replied Dave.

"Nice one, Dave," smirked Jonah.

Most of the other teams seemed to be listed less formally.

"Anyway," said Dave, "MID(i) are:

Barney Appleton (b) Rashid Trumper (c) Alan Cooke and (d) Karen Stoker" They had all heard of Karen Stoker. Who hadn't?

She was the current European Ladies Champion. Rowley knew Rashid Trumper, a fine angler. No one knew any of the others personally.

"Right," said Dave, "don't know any of this lot, but their recent form is brill. SE(ii) are: (a) Nobby Owen (b) Dave Parker (c) Charlie Hoskins and (d) Billy Suggs. At the mention of Charlie Hoskins' name, Jonah's balls froze and his penis went into wrinkled retreat. Jonah instinctively placed a protective hand on his wedding tackle.

"You okay Jonah?" asked Sid, "You look as if you've seen a ghost."

"Yeah," said Jonah, "had a bit of business with one of them boys a while back. I'll tell you about it some time." The others could sense something was up, but they pursued it no further.

Fortunately, Charlie Hoskins had no idea that J.A. Carter of NW(i) was Jonah Carter the ex-employee who had humped his missus, Glenda. Not yet anyway.

Jonah's gleaming white, one year old, Ford Transit Diesel purred resplendently at the ferry terminal of Liverpool's Pier Head. He had bought it for a song of course and it was loaded to the gunwales with his and his team-mate's fishing gear. Jonah had had an extra seat, complete with its own seatbelt, fitted in the back, so that all four of them could travel in comfort. In pride of place, harnessed to the dashboard, was a beautiful silver trophy. It had been presented to them the night before in The Spit and Sawdust. It came as quite a surprise.

At 10pm precisely, Pam had winked to Neil Taylor, the pub's landlord. Neil then slipped on a 'Queen' CD and, at volume 10, rocking the roof to its rafters, Freddie Mercury hammered out, 'We are the Champions'. This was the cue for every one else in the pub to stand up, wave their arms, and sing in unison with Freddie. The crowd walked towards their team, NW(i), who sat bewildered and proud. When the belting rock song had finished, Neil Taylor brought the assembled throng to order and announced.

"This is just a small trophy from all of us. It's to say how proud we are that this pub's fishing team is representing the whole of the Northwest of England in 'The Big One', over in Ireland. Well done lads!"

Applause and cheers rang out. Dave Tonks swallowed hard past the lump in his throat. Neil, the landlord, walked towards Rowley, the most senior team member, shook his hand and presented him with the trophy.

"What a wonderful surprise!" said Rowley, genuinely, and the others agreed. "Thank you all so much. We shall do our level best to win, you can be assured of that!"

The crowd laughed and cheered and backslapped their heroes, and offered them one-for-the-road drinks over and over again. The trophy was a single silver roach set on an onyx base with a silver plaque. The inscription on the plaque read:

'Rowley, Tonks, Carter and Lennon. Best in the Northwest. Good Luck Lads!'

Each team member examined the trophy adoringly in turn.

As Jonah looked at the trophy, another musical ditty sounded in his head.

When Jonah was on a roll, hooking and bagging up on roach rather than bream, he would sing:

"I'm rogering the roach, rogering the roach, ee ai adiyo, I'm rogering the roach!"

He hoped to be well and truly rogering the roach come Monday.

Next to the trophy on the dashboard of the Transit were packets of Mint Imperials, Trebor mints, Polo mints, Extra Strong mints and sticks of peppermint chewing gum. Jonah, Rowley and Dave all hoped that Sid might take the hint and do something about his bad breath.

The jaws of The Super Seacat yawned open and in rolled the Ford Transit. Jonah drove with Rowley and Sid up front. Dave rode shotgun in the back, with his nose buried in the latest fishing magazine. After parking on the ferry, they all jumped out and headed for the 'first class' lounge. They ordered early morning 'hairs of the dog' pints of ale and full English breakfast each. Whilst breakfast was being prepared, they took their drinks, stood on the deck of the Seacat, and watched the Liverpool skyline diminish in its wake.

Rowley called for a toast. He held his pint up in the direction of the city they were leaving.

"Here's to Liverpool," he said, "soon to be home to The All England Rod and Line Champions!"

"I'll drink to that," said Jonah, and all four friends clinked their pint pots together then each took a hefty swig of ale and cheered.

"Breakfast is served, gentlemen," said the bar steward, and NW(i) went back to the first class lounge to eat. Very few passengers had upgraded and thankfully there were no screaming children to contend with. After breakfast Rowley and Jonah each opted to browse the newspapers. Rowley busied himself with The Guardian crossword while Jonah scanned the tits of the day in The Daily Sport. Sid stretched out for some shut-eye and, in between checking the growing progress of the boil on his left knee, Dave re-read his fishing magazine.

Rowley was approached by a smart young man in his late twenties. He carried a notebook and pen in his hand and had a Nikon AF camera slung around his neck.

"Hello," he said, "Gordon Hockings, sports reporter, Liverpool Echo."

"How do you do," said Rowley, and they shook hands.

"You're NW(i), from The Spit and Sawdust, Freshfield," said Gordon.

47

"The very same," replied Rowley.

"May I do a short article for the Echo? You've become local sports celebrities," asked Gordon.

"By all means," said Rowley.

Rowley gave Gordon a short pen sketch of himself and the other members of the team. He explained how they had come together as a team and outlined their success over the past four seasons, culminating in their qualification for 'The Irish Match' at Pitts Reservoir, St. Helens a few weeks previously.

"Cheers," said Gordon, "I'll need a photograph, is that okay?"

"Surely," confirmed Rowley.

Much to Sid's initial chagrin, who had to be shaken awake, the Fab Four posed smiling in the first class lounge of the Super Seacat.

"Hang on," said Jonah, "something's missing."

Jonah went back to the Transit for the trophy they had been presented at The Spit and Sawdust the previous evening. In the following Monday's sports section of the Liverpool Echo the article appeared, together with a photograph of all four heroes and their trophy. The headline read: 'Local team competes for The All England Rod and Line Championship this week in Ireland. Good luck lads!'

After four hours on the Irish Sea, the team was back in the Ford Transit as the Super Seacat docked in Dublin. For Rowley the beauty of Dublin was the lack of high-rise development. This magnificent city still had a parochial charm despite its dynamic vibrancy and culture. It still concerned him, however, how all ferry traffic had to funnel its ways from the docks, cross over the River Liffey, and through the heart of the city, before being able to disperse to all points of the compass. Rowley thought, not for the first time, that Dublin needed a ring road system that started at the docks. He hoped that the Irish government and the European Commission would think likewise.

After seemingly stopping at every single traffic light in Dublin, the Ford Transit had finally made it to the outskirts of the city, and was now heading WNW along the road, which would lead to Jamestown. At the first major set of traffic lights along this road, as if by magic, the windscreen of the Ford Transit was doused with soapy water and a Romanian immigrant diligently appeared to swish his squeegee over it and then demand two Euros for the job.

"Just give him one," said Rowley.

"I'll fackin' give him one in a minute!" exclaimed Jonah, who had been startled by the sudden appearance of the windscreen cleaner.

"Steady on, he's only trying to earn a crust," said Rowley, who slipped the East European a single Euro.

Generally immigrants bewildered the Irish. This was a new phenomenon for them. The greatest Irish export, except for the Guinness, had been people. Over the past two centuries they had left the harsh realities of life in Ireland for pastures new. Some to England and Scotland but most escaped to further flung fields, especially America. Here was a nation of three million, two million of them encamped in Dublin, with some twenty million souls declaring themselves Irish-Americans, living on the other side of the Atlantic. Their Celtic seed had been scattered far and wide.

However, now, in the 21st century, Ireland was a rich European nation, with an indigenous population having to come to terms with the different cultures of the immigrants now flooding into their country. At the same traffic lights an indignant Dubliner had demanded of his East European windscreen washer:

"Will ya feck off, ya little eejit! I only just washed it meself this mornin'!" and had zoomed off, on the green light, in his brand new BMW. Here was a nation on the up, and good luck to them. Although it had to be said they were glad not to win the latest Eurovision Song Contest. Their success in that had become somewhat of a national embarrassment.

While Jonah concentrated on the driving, Rowley chatted to Sid in the front of the Ford Transit, while Dave snored contentedly in the back. Rowley kept the conversation with Sid to a minimum, as his halitosis was eye-wateringly pungent that afternoon.

The Irish countryside rolled by. Irish fields were characteristically dotted with random outgrowths of trees. The only crop to be seen was the mighty potato, that lover of acidic, boggy soils, and the only beasts were cattle and horses. The Irish now owned huge beautiful cottages, mostly single story, and painted in the most tasteful of pastel shades. Quite often these new abodes stood in the same grounds as the original tiny cottage, which had been left in peace to fall into dereliction.

There were precious few old vehicles on the new Irish roads. Brand new, or nearly new Opels, Mercedes, BMW's, Fords, Peugeots, Renaults and Fiats were, at last, the property of Europe's nouveau riche. Even the agricultural vehicles, once a target for cruel jokes, were now fresh off the production lines of JCB and Massey-Ferguson. Ireland seemed to resonate with hope, progress and success. Rowley smiled to himself. He loved the Irish, yet he knew that, despite their deserved wealth and optimism, they would never lose their charm and warmth. Such qualities are eternal.

Just over an hour into their journey, it was time to stop at 'Mother Hubbard's' for lunch and a cup of tea. They could also rotate the seating with Rowley driving, Jonah and Dave up front and Sid in the back. With Sid in the back his mates could stop rattling the bags of mints.

"Hello boys," said Molly, the owner of Mother Hubbard's café, "and what'll ye be havin'?" And, even though it was lunchtime, they all opted for the full Irish Breakfast, with huge steaming mugs of strong tea.

"'Tis the best choice you've made!" declared Molly, who then disappeared only to reappear twenty minutes later with four enormous Irish Breakfasts and the steaming mugs of tea.

An hour after Mother Hubbard's, and the Ford Transit drew onto the drive of 'The Shoal of Bream Lodge, Shannonside, Jamestown.

Bernadette Clancy stood on her stoop with her pinny on and her arms folded. As Jonah climbed out of the van she offered him a huge smile and a wicked wink. More would be in the offing during the week. Jonah had a game plan for his landlady.

Chapter 7

D.I. Steve Kendall and Sergeant John Broadbent sat by the large front window of Quinn's Bar, sipping Smithwick's bitter whilst scanning the entrance of The Sligo International Bank on the opposite side of the street.

They had expertly followed Brendan McHugh's Opel Astra, not a mean feat in a ropy VW Caravanette, and had parked in the same car park some 100m down the street. Kendall was sure that McHugh and his associates would be passing counterfeit money at the bank. After mincing around, like two gays on the pull for ten minutes, they had then decided to take refuge in Quinn's Bar. Kendall was positive McHugh would show up.

A few minutes later an ancient Ford Transit Diesel emblazoned with the legend 'DUFF SECURITY' obscured the bank entrance. Liam and Eamon Duff, resplendent in their tailor-made uniforms and peaked caps, dramatically leapt from the van and entered the bank. Their mission was to pick up sacks of Irish Punt notes—sprayed pink to render them useless as legal tender—and transport them to Dublin for incineration. This was a case of new European bureaucracy gone barmy but the Duffs didn't mind. It had secured them a decent living for the past twelve weeks and by the end of the month (May), Duff Security would revert back to Duff Transport, which would fetch and carry a far greater variety of materials from bog peat to bog rolls.

"Fuck me, here he comes," and D.I. Steve Kendall choked on his bitter. Brendan McHugh strode purposefully towards the bank carrying a large canvass holdall. One of his associates had made a similar sortie two hours earlier and another would do likewise two hours later.

"Right!" exclaimed Kendall to Sgt Broadbent, "you keep your eyes peeled here, and I'll go and change some traveller's cheques and find out what the fuck he's up to."

"Okay boss," said the sergeant.

In the back office of the bank Liam Duff had made an incredible discovery.

"Holy Mary and Joseph will ya look at this!" said Liam Duff, pushing his peaked cap to the back of his head, and spreading out two 20 Punt notes side by side on the counter of the bank.

"Look at what?" asked Eamon Duff, Liam's brother and co-director of 'Duff Security'.

"They're identical!" exclaimed Liam.

"Of course they are ya daft eejit," said Eamon, "they're both 20 Punt notes."

"No Eamon, I mean they are IDENTICAL! Look at the serial numbers!" said Liam. Eamon looked closely at the two Irish banknotes.

"Feck me!" he said, "we must 'phone the Garda. One of dem's a fake!" Liam rubbed the palm of his hand across his forehead and stared vacantly for a few moments.

"We will not," he said.

"Have ya gone barmy man?" said Eamon, "'tis the fraud you're looking at here!"

"Look," said Liam, "what have we to do with these banknotes now, Eamon?"

"Well," said Eamon, "they've been sprayed with the pink dye, so we've just to take them to Dublin for the burning."

"That's right," said Liam, "and if a few clever bog-trotters are now Euro-millionaires, who gives a shite? Good luck to them. The Government can afford it. Jesus we're the richest country in Europe!"

"I don't get it," said Eamon.

"Ireland is on schedule to be 100% 'Euro' by the end of the month," said Liam, "and I'll not be lettin' this," Liam pointed to the twin banknotes, "upset the feckin' applecart and make us look like a bunch of thick 'Micks'!"

"Sure and you've a point there," said Eamon.

"Keep it under your hat," said Liam seriously.

Eamon looked from side to side and then quickly took both the notes and put them under his hat.

D.I. Kendall sat at a corner desk in The Sligo International Bank dutifully signing ten traveler's cheques as Brendan McHugh waited third in line at the first teller's station. D.I. Kendall joined the queue just as Brendan McHugh reached into his holdall and methodically placed bundles of 20 Punt notes onto the counter. There were 2500 notes totaling 50000 counterfeit Punts in all.

"Heavens above, is it the lottery you have won!" exclaimed the teller cheerily.

"I wish," said Brendan calmly. "Me business is buying and selling cash-in-hand, and I thought it was about time to go European and get me Euros."

"Approximately how much do you have there sir," asked the teller.

"No' approximately' about it. There's exactly 50000 Punts, all 20's," said Brendan.

"And there's a pretty penny," smiled the teller.

To be sure," replied Brendan who was feeling increasing animosity towards the pimply youth on the other side of the counter. He had, of course deigned to stay calm at all times when exchanging the notes.

"I have to random test some of the notes you understand sir, it's a set precautionary procedure."

"Do what you must," said Brendan.

The teller selected ten notes at random and, one by one placed them inside a UV scanning machine. The indicator light remained green ten times. This was due to the signals from the short wave frequency jamming device Brendan had in the breast pocket of his shirt. It cost $7500. Money well spent. As far as the teller was concerned the notes were genuine. Brendan McHugh afforded himself the briefest of smiles.

"All in order," said the teller. He then placed bundles of the notes into the rapid counting machine. It took just over four minutes to ascertain there were exactly 2500 of the same denomination notes. The teller then calculated the conversion to Euros, a sum just short of 75000.

"So how would you be wanting that sir?"

"Cash," replied Brendan McHugh coldly.

Tis a tidy sum to be carrying on your person sir. Are you sure you wouldn't prefer to open an account and deposit it here?"

"Is there a law against a man carrying cash?"

"Well of course not sir," said the teller swallowing hard.

"Then cash I'll have," said McHugh. Sensing the young man's unease he added, "But don't be sending your mates to be mugging me now!" The unease was broken and the teller laughed. He then disappeared to the bank vault and reappeared in less than five minutes with piles of brand new Euros. The majority of them were bundled in 5000 Euro wads, which McHugh arranged methodically in his holdall.

"Have a nice day," said McHugh.

"I will," replied the teller.

"Follow the cunt," Kendall whispered into his mobile.

Sergeant Broadbent swiftly downed the remains of his pint and headed for the door only to bump into McHugh on his way in.

"Guinness, please," ordered McHugh loudly.

"Oh fuck it," Broadbent said under his breath and after hovering around for a few seconds decided to join his boss.

Broadbent bumped into Kendall in the doorway of the bank.

"Clumsy sod!"

"Sorry boss."

"Where is he?" enquired Kendall rubbing his left thigh that Broadbent had just inadvertently kneed.

"Same bar we were in."

"Never mind, the evidence we need will soon be in that," and D.I. Kendall pointed to Duff Security's Transit, "and come hell or high water we are gonna get it!"

"What the bollocks is going on Steve?" asked John.

"That bastard McHugh is passing counterfeit Punts and cashing in big-time with Kosher Euros. I should have twigged it earlier. What a fucking brilliant scam! The notes get dye-sprayed and incinerated in Dublin. All the fucking evidence ends up in smoke in less than 24 hours. He's hit the Mother Lode with this one! God only knows how he's done it but he has seemingly made REAL punts. I saw them with my own eyes pass the UV scanning test. The only traceable fake bit must be the serial numbers. We've got to nail this toerag!"

"And just how do you intend to do that Steve?"

Pointing to the Duff brother's van D.I. Steve Kendall, Metropolitan Police, calmly announced, "We are going to hij

"Have you lost your fucking marbles Steve! You cannot be seriously considering blagging a bloody security van!"

"Calm down John. All we're gonna do is convince a couple of Micks to part with a stash of useless currency so we can examine it at our leisure. It's the only hard evidence we can get at the moment. Fuck only knows where the hardware is for making the notes, for all we know it may be dismantled or destroyed already."

"You're off your trolley Steve!"

"Listen John, what have these Micks got to lose? Fuck all is what. We can even pay them for their troubles don't you see?"

"No, I fucking well don't see Steve! Two British cops are committing a felony in a country where they have no jurisdiction. It's fucking mental!"

Nonetheless, in his heart, Sergeant John Broadbent knew he would go along with it. He also knew his boss would stop at nothing in apprehending Brendan McHugh. For D.I. Steve Kendall this was deeply personal.

"Four O'clock and me nephew Sean is playing in the Gaelic Football County finals and I'm stuck in a fecking van watching the mansion of a mad rich Englishwoman. 'Tis enough to make you want to spit!" exclaimed P.C. Patrick Kelsey, Wexford County Garda.

"'Tis our job Paddy, now shut your gob and have a turn on the binoculars I've got to take me a leak," and Inspector Kieran O'Brien passed the binoculars to Paddy, unzipped his pants and pissed through the open passenger side window of the Mercedes Sprinter.

Martha D'Arcy and her associates knew they were under surveillance. She also knew that she was to meet her contact in Coleraine, Northern Ireland, and pick up the Semtex. He would only deal with her personally, no one else. It would be easy to deceive a couple of Irish coppers.

Martha D'Arcy and Kathleen Connolly wandered into the garden casually chatting together.

"'Tis her, the mad woman in the garden with another woman!" shouted the excited P.C. Kelsey. Inspector O'Brien rushed to take the binoculars off Paddy.

"Will you put it away for Christ's sake!" shouted Paddy pointing to Kieran's dick, which was still dangling from his open fly.

"Oh shut up!" said Kieran, and on focusing the field binoculars announced, "Martha D'Arcy and none other than Kathleen Connolly!"

Paddy still didn't like the look of Kieran's dick.

Martha and Kathleen strolled aimlessly around the top lawn. Martha wore a vivid green anorak with the hood down, a pair of black dungarees and a huge pair of brown leather boots. In contrast Kathleen wore a blue denim jacket, a yellow jumper, faded denim jeans and white trainers. The two women spoke for about ten minutes and then went back inside. Twenty minutes later Kathleen Connolly emerged wearing a vivid green anorak with the hood up, black dungarees and huge brown leather boots. She sauntered over to the Range Rover, started it up and drove off. Thirty seconds later Inspector O'Brien and P.C. Kelsey were in discrete pursuit. Kathleen would lead them a merry dance for hours.

Martha D'Arcy tucked her riding leathers into black boots, zipped up her black leather jacket and pulled on a black aerodynamic helmet. She straddled the one-litre Yamaha motorbike, turned the ignition, revved the throttle and was zooming off to Coleraine in a twinkling.

Chapter 8

Jonah Carter's gleaming Ford Transit crunched to a halt in the driveway of 'The Shoal O'Bream' boarding house, and Team NW(1) got out.

"Welcome boys," said Bernadette Clancy cheerily, "did ye have a good crossing?"

"Blindin', Bernadette, absolutely blindin' gel. You look as gorgeous as ever," smarmed Jonah. Bernadette laughed beautifully.

"I see you've still got the blarney about you," she said.

"Never lost it darlin'. Here let me introduce you to the team." Jonah gave Rowley a back slap.

"This is Rowley a very cultured man who never loses a big fish."

"Pleased to meet you Rowley," and Bernadette extended her hand.

"Likewise (and boy what a snorting pair of tits)," said Rowley shaking Bernadette's hand, making the aforementioned tits wobble in their cups.

"And here's our Sid, brilliant on the rivers and a bit of a ladies man may I add."

"Alright love," said Sid and as Bernadette shook his hand she instantly held her breath as the first whiff of his halitosis watered her eyes.

"Last, but definitely not least, big Dave, our diamond in the rough."

"Hiya," said Dave as he simultaneously scratched the boil on his knee, blushed and shook Bernadette's hand.

"Well now," announced Bernadette, brushing the backs of her hands down her pinny, then folding her arms under her gigantic bosom, "the sheds in the garden have the fridges for your bait and there's a drying room for your waterproofs and nets. Bring your personal luggage in and I'll show you to your rooms. Two doubles is all I have. Will that be okay?"

"Absolutely. I'm with Dave, Rowley and Sid you okay together?" asked Jonah.

"Yeah, no probs," said Sid.

"Perfection," added Rowley who inwardly cringed at the thought of Sid's body odor coupled with rampant halitosis and nocturnal monotonic farting. "Can't win them all," thought Rowley.

Thankfully each double room had two beds and Rowley quickly bagged the bed next to the window, which would remain open for the duration of the stay.

It took just short of an hour to unload the van; set out their tackle in the sheds provided and organize their personal effects in their rooms.

Jonah sidled into the kitchen as Bernadette was making the team cups of tea and ham sandwiches.

"Not got yourself married again then gel?" inquired Jonah as he slid his arm around Bernadette's waist and impishly tweaked her left nipple through her blouse.

"No more husbands for me," smiled Bernadette as she busied herself with the sandwiches. The excitement had coursed through her body with the wetness coming the instant her nipple was pinched. "Mind you I believe I can still give a young cockney a run for his money!"

"Oh that you can," whispered Jonah into Bernadette's right ear. The man in Bernadette's boat sat up, resurrected and started to throb. She crossed her legs, clenched her thighs, bit her lip and swallowed hard.

"Be off with you now. Have this tea and sandwiches. I suppose you'll have to order your bait today."

"Indeed we do my love," said Jonah as Rowley breezed into the kitchen-diner.

"Well now Rowley, sit yourself down and have this morsel. It will put you on a bit before your evening meal. I'll call the others." Bernadette bustled out of the kitchen and called up the stairs, "Sid and Dave come and have your tea and a bite."

"Big girl!" observed Rowley.

"You don't know the half of it my son. Insatiable shag of a lifetime, but I've got her measure this time around," smiled Jonah.

"How's that then?" asked Rowley.

Jonah fished around in his inside pocket and brought out a folded tissue. He carefully unfolded it to reveal a single blue pill.

"What is it?" asked Rowley.

"Viagra," smiled Jonah.

"Surely you of all people have no need for that!"

"I do with this gel, believe me! Anyway it's a case of professional pride." Jonah winked, re-wrapped his permanent erection pill and slid it back into his pocket.

"I see," said Rowley, who didn't see at all.

After their tea and a bite to eat, the Fab Four trundled off to the bait shop.

The bell on the door tinkled as Jonah and the team walked into the bait shop. The bait shop was owned and run by an Irishman known as Kelly the Kraut. Kelly Gruntfahrt suffered derision all his life from the name he had inherited. Kelly's father, Herman von Gruntfahrt had been a WW two Mescherschmidt fighter pilot who, having been hounded by an RAF Hurricane in August 1940, had crash-landed his aeroplane in Ireland. Herman had run out of fuel and had skillfully guided his plane to a bone shaking wing-shattering halt in a Cork potato field. He surrendered to the

Irish, denounced his Nazi fatherland and the Irish, being neutral, allowed him to stay as long as he behaved himself.

In 1951 he married a local girl Sinead Kelly, and in 1952 along came Kelly junior. He was their only child. In 1960 Herman was awarded Irish citizenship and lived a quiet yet industrious life as a dairy farmer up until his death in 1996. Herman's wake had been a colorful affair and he was laid to rest in his pilots uniform, his Iron Cross (1st and 2nd class) and his certificate of Irish citizenship. The coffin was draped in the German Imperial flag and the Irish tricolor. He had been a well-loved immigrant.

"Hey grunt and give us a fart you old Irish kraut!" bawled Jonah.

Kelly Gruntfahrt smiled resignedly. He had heard it all before.

"Jonah Carter, well I'll be. You keep turning up like a bad penny. How y' doin'?" asked Kelly.

"Couldn't be better old son."

"Well surely be," said Kelly the Kraut, "you've made it to the big one indeed, and I'll be thinkin' you've a helluva chance you knowin' the local waters and all."

"Exactly my son, and your excellent bait will be our trump card."

"I see you're as full of the bullshit as ever."

Jonah introduced his team-mates to Kelly and recounted the tale of Herman the German, his father.

"So you see lads I have a touch of the master race in me blood," said Kelly, laughing.

Indeed he had. Like his dad, Kelly was a fine Aryan specimen. He stood 6 feet 3 inches and had a radiance of blonde hair now streaked with white as he approached his 51st year. His eyes were a steel blue and he had the body of a fit light heavyweight. He had married Hannah Carragher and sired no fewer than six healthy Gruntfahrts all of them clones of their dad. His four sons and two daughters had in turn suffered all the grunting farting nasty Nazi jibes yet survived to become well balanced Irish-Teutonic Catholics. In truth the local community was proud of its Germanic hybrids.

Kelly's eldest son Oliver Gruntfahrt who had been selected to play Rugby Union for the Irish national team acquired the icing on the parochial cake.

"Well now boys," said Kelly, "what'll be your pleasure with regard to the bait?"

"Right," said Jonah, "for the course of the match we'll need 8 gallons of maggots, reds and whites mixed; 8 gallons of your best casters: 50 kilos of breadcrumb; 48 cans of hemp seed and 48 cans of sweet corn. We've brought our own additives."

"No problem at all," said the Kraut, "my boy Aidan will ferry it up to your digs. He'll stock the fridges in the sheds."

"Blindin' Kelly," said Jonah who then paid for the bait with his credit card.

"Did you know that another of the teams is staying locally? They're arriving from London tomorrow," said Kelly.

"That's news," said Jonah who secretly prayed it wasn't Charlie Hoskins' team.

"Mary's Bar tonight then Kelly. The drinks are on us," said Jonah.

"And I'll hold you to it," said the Kraut.

Chapter 9

The Duff Security Diesel Transit belched black exhaust fumes into the air vents of the pursuing VW Caravanette. They only had 10km on a country lane before the Duffs joined the motorway to Dublin. Kendall and Broadbent would have to act soon.

"Okay John, pull along side, roll your window down and tell them their exhaust is hanging off and they should stop," instructed Kendall.

"But their exhaust isn't hanging off, Steve."

"For fucks sake John just do it! We can negotiate. 200 Euros apiece for their Punts."

"Here goes nothing," said John Broadbent who pulled along side the fuming Ford, and rolled his window down.

"Hey mate!" shouted John.

Liam Duff looked suspiciously at the English tourist.

"What?" he mouthed through his closed window.

"Stop!" said John Broadbent, pointing to the rear of the Duffs' van, "your exhaust is hanging off."

Liam turned to Eamon and asked, "did you not have the van serviced last week?"

"I did."

"Was the exhaust okay?"

"It was fine, but the exhaust valves are buggered."

Liam turned to face the English tourist and bawled through his closed window. "Feck off! We're on Government business and can't stop for anyone!" With that Liam slammed the accelerator to the floorboards and the Ford lumbered up to 52mph, its top speed.

"Ram him!" ordered D.I. Kendall.

"Fuck off!" replied Sgt. Broadbent.

"Ram the fucker John, come on!"

"No way Steve, this has gone way too far!"

"Alright, alright, just overtake him slowly then."

Sgt. Broadbent did as instructed, and the moment the Caravanette had overtaken the Ford, without warning, D.I. Kendall pulled hard left on the steering wheel.

"What the f . . . ," was all that Broadbent could utter as the Caravanette slewed in front of the Ford and instinctively he slammed on the anchors. Just as instinctively, Liam pulled hard left to avoid crashing into the tourists' vehicle and hit the curb at 52mph. Momentarily all four wheels of the Ford Transit were airborne only to be stuck two feet deep in a muddy ditch two seconds later. The engine cut out. It would never restart.

"You fucking headcase Steve!"

"Whatever. Come on John."

The two British cops jumped out of the Caravanette and raced towards the Ford Transit.

"You okay?" asked Steve through the passenger side window.

Liam and Eamon were terrified and had curled up under the dashboard.

"Feck off you maniac!" shouted Liam.

"I know it looks bad," implored D.I. Kendall "we don't wish you any harm. We'll pay you for the Punts, we need them as evidence. We're British policemen. Come on lads out you get please, let's talk."

"British policemen my arse," said Eamon to Liam. "They've more than likely got a way of removing the pink dye and spending the money is what I'm thinking."

"Jesus, you've a point there Eamon."

"Did you pick up your mobile phone Liam?"

Liam's face lit up as he snatched up his mobile from the door well. He switched it on. It bleeped, registered 'flat battery' and instantly became immobile.

"Feck it all!" cursed Liam.

"We'll just sit tight. The doors and windows are reinforced so they can't get in anyway," said Eamon.

"Look lads believe me this is no big deal," said Kendall, "we'll give you 400 Euros for the Punts, they're useless anyway."

"Feck off!" was Liam's eloquent reply.

"Fucking thick Micks," muttered Kendall. "Right John, the wheel brace!"

"You're not going to try and break in for God's sake!"

"Too fucking true John."

"Christ almighty," moaned John.

D.I. Steve Kendall hammered and banged at the back doors of the Ford Transit in an attempt to force them open. Liam's heart sank and his mind went blank. Eamon had a plan. He reached into the glove compartment of the van and pulled out an aerosol lighter fuel canister, his penknife and lighter, and a huge spanner. As Liam was shouting profanities and assuring the Brits who were trying to break into his van that he had telephoned the Garda who were on their way that very minute, Eamon acted.

With the spanner he smashed the small adjoining window between the front and rear compartments of the van. He then punctured the lighter fuel canister and threw it hissing into the back of the van. He closely followed this with the vans' tax disc, which he had set alight. WHOOOOSH!

"Jesus Mary and Joseph what on Earth are you doing man!" shouted Liam.

"Me job," said Eamon, "I'm burning the Punts so they can't be stolen."

At this juncture D.I. Kendall had managed to wrench open the back doors of the Ford ever so slightly. The influx of the extra oxygen-carrying air turned the smoldering punts into a livid inferno. Flames shot through the gap between the doors and singed Kendall's eyebrows.

"You fucking maniacs!" yelled Kendall clutching his forehead.

"You feckin' maniac!" yelled Liam to Eamon.

"Feck off!" yelled Eamon to everyone.

Liam and Eamon were quickly engulfed in black smoke. Coughing and choking they simultaneously kicked open the doors of their van. They jumped into the ditch, struggled out of the mud and ran blindly across an open field. Liam cursed Eamon at every stride. Eamon's hat flew off as did the two 20 Punt notes he had hidden there.

Duff's van seemed to audibly breathe in the extra air afforded by the open doors and in a twinkling the whole van was well ablaze.

"Fuck this for a game of darts!" shouted Kendall, "the fucking fuel tank could blow!"

John Broadbent leapt into the VW Caravanette and started her up. D.I. Kendall ran towards the vehicle but slipped and fell skinning both elbows and knees. As he lay in the road momentarily cursing his luck manna arrived from heaven. Two 20 Punt notes drifted out of the ether and landed side by side in front of his nose. Kendall instinctively looked at the serial numbers.

"Fuck me they're identical!"

"Get your arse in here pronto!" shouted Broadbent.

D.I. Kendall snatched up the notes and leapt into the Caravanette. They had traveled only 50 metres before the Ford Transit's Diesel fuel tank ignited. The Transit was propelled vertically some 3 meters into the air before unceremoniously crashing back down into the muddy ditch where it burned away merrily.

"Got some hard evidence John, what a stroke of luck! Put your foot down we've got to ditch this Caravanette."

Sergeant John Broadbent said nothing he was certain that his boss had become permanently deranged.

Liam and Eamon sat gasping in the middle of an Irish field. They watched as the ancient German Caravanette disappeared around a bend. Their own vehicle was now a smoldering wreck.

"'Tis probably not the best time to be telling you," said Eamon.

"Tell me what?" asked Liam.

"I forgot to post off the insurance on the van."

Chapter 10

Jonah Carter led the team into Mary's Bar.

"Hello Mary my love, how are you?" said Jonah genuinely.

"Jonah Carter. Now there's a sight for sore eyes," said Mary smiling. "Mind you I should have guessed it as the big match is almost upon us. I'm fine Jonah. And yourself?"

"All the better for seeing you."

"Still got the silver tongue then. What'll it be?"

"Three pints of the black stuff and a pint of Smithwick's please Mary." With that Jonah introduced the rest of the team to Mary.

Mary Finucane pulled the pints for the Englishmen and smiled to herself. Mary Finucane was 84 years old. As a highly educated young woman she had been a proactive political activist and had served time in a British prison. She had also sired 11 children and buried 3 husbands. She stood a whisper short of 5 foot and although her fiery red hair had almost all faded to grey, there was still sufficient colour there to offset her brilliant green eyes. Like good red wine Mary had mellowed over the years and all that knew her respected her valuable counsel.

When local problems arose, Mary's advice was the first to be sought. On the rare occasion her advice was not heeded, disaster usually ensued. This was the case with 'the famous arch'. Jamestown was named after the second king of England and Ireland with that name. He was a bumbling monarch in truth, but a good Catholic all the same. In the 17th century an archway across the road had been erected in his honour. In 1970 the local council had wanted to knock it down in order to allow high-sided vehicles through. Mary's advice had been emphatic.

"No, you'll regret it if you do."

The arch was knocked down anyway but in the late 80's and through the 90's as European Ireland expanded its motorway system, it became apparent that the demolition had been unnecessary. When the council, in their wisdom, decided to rebuild the archway with its original stone, it was found that the 17th century masonry had been used in the foundations of a bar. A rich piece of Irish history had been buried in the name of the Guinness family.

Mary, of course, had been right. She was, however, not of a nature to say 'I told you so'.

It took Mary six minutes to pull the three pints of Guinness. A squirt in each pint pot was followed by a measured wait as the rich brew settled. When the liquid almost reached the top of each glass, the creamy head of the stout was sliced off with a plastic spatula and Mary dribbled in the last of it up to the imperial pint marker.

In transition to a European nation, Ireland still had mixed measurements. Ale was sold in pints not litres, yet spirits were sold in 25 or 50ml shots. Traffic signs had not finally converted either. Distances between towns and villages were given in both miles and kilometres. Jonah had once asked Bernadette how far it was from Jamestown to Carrick.

"Would that be in miles or kilometres, Jonah?"

"Miles if you like," said Jonah.

"In miles it's about half an hour," she said.

A better answer could not be given.

The temperature of Mary's Guinness was perfect, cool never cold.

"There you go," said Mary handing over the full pint pots, "shall I put it on the slate for you Jonah?"

"If you would Mary, I'll settle up before closing time. By the way, when is closing time?"

"'Tis the same as ever Jonah, we close when you leave."

"How civilized!" enthused Rowley, "cheers Mary."

"Your health," said Mary to Rowley, and as an aside to Jonah, "I believe you're staying up at 'The Shoal O'Bream' with Bernadette Clancy again."

"Right again Mary," said Jonah.

"She's a fine woman," said Mary, and fixing her beautiful green eyes on Jonah added, "she'll serve you well." Mary and Jonah smiled knowingly at each other.

"You never miss a trick do you Mary?"

A middle-aged blonde Adonis strode into the Bar.

"Hey up, it's Kelly," said Sid, "he's not to pay for any ale tonight Mary, put it on our tab love."

"I will," said Mary.

Martha D'Arcy parked her one-litre Yamaha outside 'Clohessy and Sons, Funeral Directors, Coleraine.' As expected the gold and black doors were open and she walked in carrying a small handbag. It seemed apt that she was dressed all in black. She had come to meet with Michael Clohessy Jnr., a very black-hearted man indeed.

Michael Clohessy Jnr. dealt in death, both as a trade and a pastime. He was an independent agent now after being expelled from the Real IRA for gross insubordination. His contacts, however, didn't care as long as they received top dollar for their arms and explosives. Clohessy's merchandise didn't come cheap but it was invariably the best available.

Martha entered Michael's office. She took off her helmet and placed it with her small handbag on the large oak table. She shook her grey hair, sat down in a finely upholstered chair, crossed her legs and waited for Clohessy. It was two minutes to 8pm. Their meeting was scheduled for 8pm.

Michael Clohessy Jnr. was an exact man. At precisely 8pm he entered his office carrying a smart attaché case and locked the door behind him. Clohessy was a dapper, clean-cut man on the exterior. At 35 his neatly trimmed jet—black hair was greying slightly at the temples. He was short, standing only 5ft 7ins. He had angular features an olive complexion and dark brown eyes. In truth he looked more Italian than Irish. He wore black patent leather shoes, dark grey slacks and a black polo neck sweater.

"Hello Martha," he said, coldly offering his hand in welcome.

"Michael," said Martha with a nod of her head. She took Michael's hand and shook it briefly. She sat back in her seat and shuffled it closer to the oak desk. Michael stood opposite and clicked open the attaché case.

"To business," he said.

He swiveled the open attaché case around so that Martha could examine its compartmentalized contents. Michael pointed to compartment one.

"Semtex, Czech Republic stuff, high quality, the best."

He then pointed to compartment two.

"Forty detonators."

His index finger moved on to indicate compartment three.

"Forty electronic switches. One preprogrammed SIMMs card. Detonation is controlled by mobile phone, hence the card."

Finally he pointed to compartment four.

"Five hundred meters of low-resistance 2mm copper wire. This is only necessary if you require all the detonators to fire simultaneously. They can be popped off one at a time if you prefer; in any case Kathleen Connolly will have no problem putting it all together. She's a real pro."

"Indeed she is," said Martha who then zipped open her handbag and drew out one hundred $100 bills, which she handed to Michael.

"$10000 was the agreed price?"

"It was," said Michael who methodically counted out each greenback. One currency and one denomination was all he dealt in. US dollars, $100 bills only.

Michael placed the money in a draw, clicked shut the attaché case and handed it to Martha.

"Good luck," he said and shook her hand in farewell.

Kathleen Connolly peered into the Range Rover's rear-view mirror and smiled. The Mercedes Sprinter and the two Irish coppers were still with her. She would lead them up the garden path for a few more hours sufficient for Martha to return from the North.

"I feel bad about them two Micks," said D.I. Steve Kendall.

"Did get a bit of a raw deal. Boy were they scared shitless!" and Sergeant John Broadbent chuckled at the image of the two security men bounding terrified across an open field.

"I'm paying them for their troubles anyway. I've put 400 Euros in an envelope to the Sligo International Bank care of 'Duff Security'."

"Nice one boss," said Sgt. Broadbent.

They had abandoned the VW Caravanette in a multi-story car park and had hired a 1.8 Ford Mondeo Estate. The rear seats were down and Kendall lay prostrate in the back with his field binoculars trained on Donna McHugh's cottage a 100m away.

"I'm sure the machine's in there you know John. I'd love to get my hands on it."

It wasn't and he wouldn't.

Liam and Eamon Duff recounted the sorry tale of their burned-out business to an officer of the local Garda. They gave poor descriptions of the two English would-be hijackers, but a very good description of their VW Caravanette. A policeman and an official from the Sligo International Bank had examined the husk of their van and, although they thought he was nuts, praised Eamon for his heroic deed.

"Still, you can claim on the insurance," said P.C. Donovan.

"Bit of a sore point that," said Eamon gingerly.

Liam became morose. He cheered up four days later when he opened up the anonymous envelope sent via the Sligo International Bank. 400 Euros was a damn sight more than their old Ford was worth.

Chapter 11

By 10 o'clock Mary's bar was heaving. All present were enjoying the 'craic', after all it was Saturday night. The Fab Four however had decided to leave come 11pm. They were out to 'reccy' all the venues the following day and they planned on an early start.

The bar had really begun to pulsate when two accomplished fiddlers, a young man and his heavily pregnant girlfriend, had flopped their woolen hats on a table and started to play and sing unannounced. As the volume of the foot-stomping clapping and singing increased, so did the volume of cash in their hats.

Mary Finucane was aided and abetted behind the bar by her two youngest granddaughters. They were beautiful girls both in their late teens. One had long black hair tied back in a ponytail and the other had an insanity of curly red hair, which danced about her shoulders.

Rowley was more interested in their tits. He had studied them closely for almost an hour now. Each pneumatic brace was tightly contoured under a black T-shirt, which had the logo FCUK emblazoned in white between the nipples.

"FCUK me," thought Rowley, "I could play with them all night!"

Rowley loved Irish bars. He smiled and breathed in the atmosphere. He liked the occasional good cigar and had one propped up in its metal tube in his shirt pocket. He had, however, already passively smoked the equivalent of a whole packet of cigarettes. Ireland was on course to become the first European nation to ban lighting up in all public places.

Steve Parker

Dirty Sid was in his element. There was nothing he enjoyed more (apart from shagging) than a good old singsong. Sid also had a terrific singing voice. When the fiddlers launched into 'Come on Eileen', Sid took centre stage on the floor of the bar and belted out the lyrics expertly. He received a thoroughly deserved round of applause at the end.

Big Dave Tonks was well pissed after four pints. He had finally given up trying to read his fishing magazine and was joining in the merriment with gusto. He gave it his best shot when the fiddlers played 'The Wild Rover'.

"And its no, nay never," bump, bump, bump bump, bump, bump, "no nay, never again," he sang waving his arms in the air as if he were down the Kop at Anfield. In fact, Teresa Finucane, the nubile redhead behind the bar had given big Dave the eye all night but he was oblivious to it. In any case Dave could only guarantee an erection if he was playing a big fish or looking at a photograph of one!

Surprisingly Jonah had been drinking well within himself. He was sticking to his game plan for Bernadette Clancy. He would service her gratuitously for five nights then give her the Viagra-induced biggie on Thursday, his last night at her digs. Professional pride demanded he succeed.

At 10:30pm Father McCartney sidled into the bar almost unnoticed. Mary Finucane did however notice him and immediately poured him a half of Guinness.

"Thank you Mary," he mouthed through the din.

Mary nodded and smiled. Fr. McCartney only ever drank half-pints. The fact that he could down twelve such measures in two hours was beside the point. Mary never charged the priest. At the age of 84 a place in heaven was fondly anticipated. After four half-pints, Father McCartney almost eclipsed dirty Sid in the singing stakes. He gave a superb rendition of the Beatles' classic 'Yesterday'. He had grown up a child of the 60's and adored all

The Beatles stuff. Sid hustled his way over to the priest who was now on his 5th half-pint.

"Hey Father, I love all the Beatles stuff too how about we do one together?"

"T'would be a delight!" said the priest.

And there it was that the assembled throng in this tiny Irish bar, saw and heard Lennon and McCartney belt out an excellent rendition of 'Ticket to Ride!'

At 11pm Jonah motioned to his mates to drink up which they did reluctantly. He had already paid Mary and had given her a hefty tip, which she appreciated. Team NW(i) belched and farted its way back to 'The Shoal O'Bream' and by 11:30 Rowley, Sid and Dave were washed and bedded.

Jonah tiptoed naked into Bernadette's room. She had been lying in bed wet and expectant for almost an hour. When Jonah entered her bedroom she breathed deeply, closed her eyes tight shut and pressed the palms of her hands into the mattress. Jonah slinked in beside her and kissed her right ear. Bernadette groaned softly and reached for Jonah's over-sized stiff member.

"Jesus!" she whispered, "a bigger boy I've yet to meet!"

"Easy gel, I've an early start in the morning so this will be no marathon."

"Sure and you're a wicked man Jonah Carter," she gasped.

Jonah kissed Bernadette full on the lips whilst fondling her enormous tits. Instantaneously her nipples became so hard you could hang washing on them.

Jonah's right hand slid across the contours of her belly and furrowed gently into her pubic hair. He then plopped two fingers into the opening of her vagina. It felt as though it had been primed with warm wallpaper paste.

"No need for foreplay then?" asked Jonah jokingly.

"Oh for heaven's sake man get on with it!" implored Bernadette.

She spread her legs and lifted up her knees so that her ankles touched each cheek of her fearful arse. Jonah oozed into delicious action giving her half a dozen long strokes.

"Oh, oh, oh, oh," she moaned.

After ten more long strokes she was on the 'edge'.

"She's incredible," thought Jonah.

"Go on, go on, go on, faster, go on!"

Jonah moved into second gear.

"Go on, go on, holy Mary and Joseph, go on, go on!"

Third gear.

"Go on, that's it, go on, go on, oh Jesus, faster Jonah!"

Fourth gear. Bernadette wrapped her legs around Jonah's arse and held the headboard with her hands. Here came the deeply penetrating short strokes.

"Go on Jonah, I'm coming I'm sure of it, go on, go on!"

Jonah had heard it all before. There was to be no overdrive tonight. He gave it 25 minutes creamed his cocoa and stopped.

"Oh Jesus Jonah don't stop please. I was nearly there I know it!" and tears welled up in Bernadette's eyes.

Jonah cupped her face in his hands, kissed her on the forehead and said, "Listen gel, I'm going to get you there and that's a promise. Believe me."

"Okay," she said breathlessly, "if it's a promise." "Guaranteed," said Jonah and, after kissing her forehead again, he hopped off into his own bedroom and listened to big Dave snoring.

Chapter 12

With the passenger seats down, D.I. Steve Kendall was lying full-length in the back of the Ford Mondeo Estate peering through his field binoculars. He, and Sergeant John Broadbent were justoutside the town of Drumod near Loch Boderg.

"So that's their little game!"

"What is?"

"Have a butcher's" and D.I. Kendall passed the binoculars to his sergeant.

Brendan McHugh was carrying 4 dark blue, heavy-duty plastic bags out to a small dinghy tethered to a rock on the edge of Loch Boderg.

The dinghy had been rowed ashore by Mick Kelly who exchanged the blue bags from his boss for 4 large red bags, which McHugh took back to his Opel. Kelly then untied the painter of his dinghy and rowed out to a large white motor launch anchored some 50m from the edge of the Loch. Sgt. Broadbent scanned the prow of the powerful motor launch to read the legend 'Zeppellin'. Draped at the stern of the boat was the German national flag.

"What's it all about chief?"

"The way I see it John is, . . . the blue bags are full of kosher Euros, and red bags are stuffed with Mickey Mouse punts. We know that these slags started in Sligo, and it's my guess they'll be cashing in the counterfeit punts all the way down to Limerick.

"Yeah, but why piss about along the Shannon waterway, why not just do it by road in cars?"

"Think about it, John."

"I am. Still don't make sense to me."

"Look, let's say The Garda get wind of this. Where's the incriminating evidence?"

"Well, the punts they've exchanged for Euros will have been sprayed and incinerated, so the real incriminating stuff is on the 'Zeppellin'."

"Precisely!"

"Precisely what?"

"Counterfeit punts and water don't mix, so, over the side with them."

"But they could have, say, a million Euros on the boat. Bit difficult to explain why."

"True John, but Euros in watertight bags plus an electronic tracking device could be dumped in the centre of any Loch, to be collected at one's leisure."

"Clever buggers," mused Sgt. Broadbent, "but why the Kraut boat?"

"The entire Shannon waterway is a favourite boating haunt for tourists, especially Germans. It's a smokescreen."

"Look chief, we've got the two identical twenty punt notes, we've seen McHugh acquire thousands of Euros . . . and now . . . this. I think it's time to call in The Garda, this is their manor after all."

"Fancy a spot of fishing John?"

"Y'wha?"

"We're going to hire a little motor cruiser and some fishing tackle and track our little friends in the 'Zeppellin'."

"Oh, for fuck's sake chief!" and Sgt. Broadbent buried his head in his hands. D.I. Steve Kendall rubbed his hands together and smiled broadly.

It was day 1 of The All England Rod and Line Championship on Loch Allen. Each captain had drawn four numbers for his team, and NW(i) had drawn well.

It was a cloudy but warm morning yet Jonah was wearing a thick woollen beany hat pulled down to his eyebrows. The collar of his denim jacket was turned up and his shoulders were hunched. Only his nose was visible.

"What the fuck's up with you Jonah?" asked Sid.

"Sahf-East two," said Jonah.

"Y Wha?" asked Sid.

"Look Sid, do us a favour and find out what pegs SE(ii) pulled. I need to know where Charlie Hoskins is."

"What's it all about Jonah?"

"Humped his missus."

"Naughty lad! Is this Hoskins hard?"

Jonah balked at the pungent whiff of Sid's bad breath.

"Could be a bit messy Sid. 'Ere, fancy a polo mint?"

"No ta. I'll go an 'ave a reccy, we don't start for another thirty minutes.

"You're a diamond my son."

Rowley had drawn the peg next to Dave Tonks. Marvelous! He would watch Dave and copy his technique right down to the size of hook and preferred hookbait. Dave was slowly drifting into his pre-match trance . . . a goodly sign.

"Hoskins is on peg 21," said Sid.

"Thank Christ!" said Jonah, who visibly relaxed and carted his gear off to peg 4.

"ALL IN!" was called at 9:00am, and twenty minutes later Jonah was into a shoal of bream. His musical repertoire followed . . .

"All I have to do is bream . . ."

"Bream lover where are you . . ."

"Have you ever seen a bream walking?" and so on.

Rowley and Dave were rogering the roach and Sid had found a very productive tench hole off some lily pads. It would prove to be an excellent day's fishing.

"ALL OUT!" was called at 2pm, and thirty minutes later the 1,2, 3 was announced. NE(i) came 3rd, MID(i) was 2nd and by a clear 37lb NW(i) were declared the winners.

More than a few ales would be drowned later, and Bernadette Clancy would receive another 9inch meat injection, courtesy the Cocky Cockney.

Inspector Kieran O'Brien together with P.C. Patrick Kelsey had tracked Martha D'Arcy to a boat yard. Their unmarked Mercedes Sprinter was parked up at 'McNally's Used Boat Yard, Athlone'. Inspector O'Brien wandered around 'McNally's' feigning interest in the sail boats.

Martha D'Arcy was haggling over the price of a powerful 35ft twin-screw motor launch.

"I bet that moves like the shit off a hot shovel," mused the inspector. The deal was struck and Martha, having made a call on her mobile phone, shook hands with McNally and marched off to the office to finalise the paperwork.

"Y see that feckin big white monster," said the inspector to P.C. Kelsey.

"I do."

"She's just feckin bought it!"

"Why would she be doin' that then?"

"Mary and Joseph I haven't got a feckin clue, but you can be as sure as Christmas that she's up to no feckin good, mark my words!"

"She could be takin a holiday."

"Patrick, I sometimes think yer brains are hid up yer arse," and just then the inspector's eyes widened in disbelief.

"Feck me! Look!"

And just then Kathleen Connolly drove into the yard in a Range Rover pulling a huge boat trailer. In less than twenty minutes the motor launch 'The Feisty Lady' was harnessed in a cradle and gently lowered onto the trailer.

Back at D'Arcyfields 'The Feisty Lady' would undergo a radical transformation.

Rowley, Sid and a rather subdued Jonah were not only enjoying the 'craic' at Mary's Bar but were also warmly reminiscing their win on Loch Allen. Dave was enjoying a mega-dump in the bog.

Just then Nobby Owen, Dave Parker, Billy Suggs and Charlie Hoskins i.e. Team SE(ii), sauntered into the bar.

Furtively peering over Rowley's shoulder, Jonah spotted his nemesis. He choked into his Guinness, slammed his pint pot on the bar, and raced off to the toilet.

Dave Tonks produced only two varieties of turd. Number One, the 'legless newt' variety, and, Number Two, the more challenging, 'Nux bar' variety. This was a Number One session and Dave sat happily on his throne reading 'The Angling Times', his trousers a crumpled atoll around his ankles.

"Anyone 'ere from NW(i)?" enquired Charlie Hoskins.

"Indeed", said Rowley.

"Charlie Hoskins," said Charlie Hoskins, who then introduced the rest of his team. Handshakes were exchanged and Rowley wondered where Jonah had disappeared to.

"Good win on Loch Allen," said Hoskins.

"Thank you," replied Rowley. Sid said nowt.

"Bit of a long shot," said Hoskins," but I was looking at your team names and was wondering if 'J. Carter' was in fact Jonah Carter from Muswell Hill, a pretty decent fisherman I used to know."

"Well, as a matter of fact . . ." started Rowley, only to be cut short by Sid's elbow in his ribs.

"No," said Sid, "he's John Carter, originally from Birmingham who now lives in Liverpool. He joined our team last season, good fisherman."

"Oh, right," said Hoskins.

"This Jonah Carter a friend of yours?" enquired Sid.

"To tell you the truth my son," said Hoskins "if I ever catch up with Jonah Carter again I'll rip his fuckin bollocks off!"

"I see," said Rowley, gulping.

Hoskins and his team then wandered over to a table and started discussing their tactics for the second match.

Rowley looked at Charlie Hoskins and shuddered. He was a brute of a man. Short, bald, and powerfully built. He sported a nose and ear ring and his arms were illustrated with the most lurid tattoos. Hoskins looked a very menacing unit indeed. 'Not to be messed with' thought Rowley.

There was one urinal and one throne in the toilet. The window was on the wall behind the throne, the door to which was locked as Dave Tonks purposefully jettisoned his third 'legless newt'.

Jonah's hands followed by his head appeared over the throne door.

"What the fuck's goin' on!" demanded Dave.

"Long story," said Jonah who had now clambered into the cubicle.

"But what the fuck . . ." implored Dave.

"Put a sock in it pal, got to go," and Jonah jumped up onto the cistern behind a bewildered Dave, opened the window and slid off into a balmy Irish night.

"What the deuce was all that about Sid," enquired Rowley.

"The tattooed nutcase has a score to settle with Jonah. He shagged his missus."

"Jesus Christ, Jonah must have a bloody death wish! We better get Dave clued up so he doesn't let the cat out of the bag."

Just then a seriously disgruntled Dave appeared suffering from a severe case of 'interrupted-dump-syndrome'.

"That fuckin maniac Jo . . ." and at that precise moment Sid slapped the palm of his hand over Dave's mouth, told him to shut up and listen. Dave shut up and listened.

"Incognito from now on," Rowley informed Jonah, "that moronic Neanderthal Hoskins could banjo the living daylights out of all of us on his own, so, from now on, here is the form."

Jonah groaned but allowed Rowley to continue.

"Balaclava and shades to be worn at all times," said Rowley, "we'll say you have a head cold and laryngitis, that way you don't have to speak to anyone."

"Bit severe, my son," whined Jonah.

"You can take your headgear and shades off when you're servicing Bernadette, come to think of it, she might like a bit of kinky sex!" and Rowley roared with laughter.

Jonah smiled resignedly but agreed to the survival plan.

Later that night when he appeared in Bernadette's bedroom sporting only a Balaclava, shades and monumental hard-on, her blood-curdling screams nearly took the roof off.

"Bollocks to this," said Jonah. He threw off his disguise and oozed himself balls deep into Bernadette's honeypot.

"Go on oh go on Jonah, 'tis lovely, I'm nearly there!"

"Here we go again," thought Jonah, pumping away vigorously. He had a plan for the teams last night. Sid and Dave would surely help.

He knew Rowley wouldn't.

From a wooded hillock behind the manor house at D'Arcyfields, Inspector O'Brien and P.C. Kelsey had a great view into the courtyard.

Resplendent on her trailer was 'The Feisty Lady' and essential modifications were well underway.

The original Perkins diesel engines had been replaced with two monster Volvo V6 car engines and the new propellers were twice the size of the originals.

"Sweet Jesus, that's one mighty powerful boat they're putting together there," and Inspector O'Brien passed the night-vision binoculars to P.C. Kelsey.

They didn't need the night-vision facility as the entire courtyard was lit up by huge flood lights as a team of mechanics-cum-engineers worked around the clock on 'The Feisty Lady'.

"Wot's dem six chimneys stickin out in front of the cockpit?" asked Kelsey.

"I've an idea they're pipe-rockets," said O'Brien, "she put the same into a Transit van in England, and blew the bejesus out of The Gloucestershire Hunt awhile back."

"Dis woman is feckin nuts!" said Kelsey.

"She's also extremely intelligent, and, yes I agree, she's terminally deranged as well."

On either side of the prow of 'The Feisty Lady' two huge holes had been expertly machine drilled, into which two long stainless steel tubes had been inserted and meticulously fitted.

"And would you mind telling me what that's all about?"

"Torpedo tubes," said O'Brien coldly.

"Feck me boss, why don't we just arrest her and her cronies?"

"She's not broken any laws yet Patrick. She's modifying her boat in her own private grounds. We could pull her over when she tows it on the road, but it would be best if she was caught in the act using the little toys she has on board. Sure and it's a risk, but one I'm willing to take, if it means we can bang this loony and her entourage away for life!"

"I'll drink to that!" exclaimed Kelsey.

"Good! Let's go and get a couple of pints of Guinness. You're payin."

P.C. Kelsey frowned but was happy to get his arse off the damp grass and onto a warm barstool.

D.I. Kendall and a less than enthusiastic Sgt. Broadbent wandered around 'McNally's Used Boat Yard, Athlone'.

"Do you hire out boats?" asked Kendall.

"I do," replied McNally, "is it just boating or a spot of fishing you'll be doin?"

"Bugger me McNally, I think you must be a mind reader."

"Thing is," continued McNally, "I also hire out fishing tackle, at very reasonable prices."

McNally showed them his recommendation. It was a 15 foot motor-sailor with an inboard diesel engine. It sat resplendent on its trailer, its rusting hull was heavily camouflaged with several coats of thick dark green paint and its name 'Leprechaun' was painted in gold, port and starboard.

"Plenty of room on her," said McNally, "the engine's quite powerful, but she can also function at a snail's pace if you fancy trolling off the back. I'll include all the tackle you need, including two strong boat rods apiece. Now for how long will you be wanting her?"

"Not too sure," said Kendall, "could we pay for, say, five days and take it from there?"

"A week is the minimum," said McNally.

"How much?"

"280 Euros."

"I'll give you 200."

"'Tis a deal!" said a delighted McNally.

Chapter 13

The four musketeers which made up team NW(i) were on the banks of the beautiful River Shannon near Jamestown. It was day two of The All England Rod and Line Championship (The 'Irish Match'). Thankfully Charlie Hoskins and SE(ii) were a good half a mile up river and, despite the day being warm and muggy, Rowley insisted that Jonah keep his balaclava and shades on.

"I'm sweating already," moaned Jonah.

"Tough," was Rowley's succinct reply, "should learn to keep your oversized appendage in your jocky shorts lad, and cut out all the talking, you're supposed to be a Brummie."

NW(i) had drawn a stretch of the magnificent River Shannon, some 80 metres in length. This took in a bend with rapids on the inside, and slower moving deeper water on the outside.

"Whatcha think Sid?" asked Dave.

Sid was in his element. He loved fishing rivers.

"Got to do this as a team," said Sid. "If pike get into this swim we're fucked, so, Rowley your goin' pikin. If there are any pike about they'll be stalking over there," and Sid pointed to an area of swaying reeds on the opposite bank. "You know the score, heavy tackle and deadbait on your hook."

"Indeed," said Rowley.

"Right Dave," said Sid, "fish the entire swim and take out the small perch, they're a fuckin' nuisance. Use pinky or red maggot."

"Ok," said Dave.

"Now Jonah," said Sid, "fish mainly on the slow side of the bend, you're after bream so groundbait it up first, you know the score."

"Alright my son," said Jonah.

"I'll fish those rapids should end up rogering the roach with a bit of luck."

Sid's plan worked. Rowley caught the first fish of the day, an 8lb pike, and with such a large predator out of the way, the rest of the swim became very productive.

Dave and Sid caught steadily but Jonah had blanked with less than an hour of the match remaining. Just then a shoal of bream moved in and started to feed on Jonah's groundbait. Brilliant!

After the 'weigh-in' NW(i) had come second, but overall they were still in the lead by some 24lbs. The eventual winners would be the team with the highest poundage over the five days.

That evening, to celebrate their success, the Team drove to a bar in Roosky. They were the only English fishermen there, which suited Jonah just fine. The 'craic' was great. There was a fiddle player and a girl on a penny whistle banging out Irish country tunes. Sid did a singing party-piece, 'The Long and Winding Road', by The Beatles, of course, for which he was warmly applauded. Sid and Dave hit the Guinness with a vengeance. Jonah stuck to the Smithwick's bitter, and Rowley, ever the designated driver, had a couple of glasses of white wine.

Jonah's performance with Bernadette later that night was affected by partial 'brewer's-droop.' It took an awful lot of blood to pump his pecker up but, nevertheless he had big plans for her later in the week.

Loch Ree at Ballykeeran. Third day of the match.

The team hauled their gear out of the back of Jonah's Ford Transit and loaded up their trolleys. Rowley attended the draw for the pegs and NW(i) were all quite close to each other on the east side of the Loch. Luckily SE(ii) were all over the place but, more importantly, Charlie Hoskins was way over on the west side. Jonah sighed with relief. He took off his shades but was thankful for the balaclava as the weather was blowing a gale directly into their faces.

"Sidewinders," declared Dave. The rest of the team agreed. Sidewinders are a brilliant invention. They are bite indicators attached to the body of the rod through which the line is passed. They enable the fisherman to keep the tip of his feeder rod in the water so it is not affected by waves or wind and the line is kept tight. If the sidewinder twitches, it's a bite. It's as simple as that. Jonah called them 'dog's dicks' but, boy, were they effective.

And, boy, did the 'dog's dicks' wag that day. All four team members bagged up, mainly on bream, and, yes, Jonah sang his entire 'bream' repertoire over and over again.

At the 'weigh-in' NW(i) came third. Their overall lead had been cut to 12lbs, but they were still in the lead and remained confident.

Inspector O'Brien and P.C. Kelsey were back at their vantage point overlooking D'Arcyfields. It was just another day watching the mad English woman. It appeared as though the final touches were being carried out on 'The Feisty Lady'.

To the bulkhead in front of the wheelhouse a loudhailer had been attached so that whoever steered the boat could use it hands-free.

"Now what's all that about?" asked P.C. Kelsey.

"I think that whatever they get up to we'll be getting a running commentary," said Inspector O'Brien.

"What do you mean by . . ." but Kelsey was cut short.

"Shut yer gob Patrick. Look at this!"

Kathleen Connolly had arrived in the Range Rover. She opened the boot. Two men unloaded what looked to be six rockets, each about two feet long.

"One for each pipe," said Inspector O'Brien.

"Y'what?" enquired P.C. Kelsey.

O'Brien looked Kelsey in the eye, frowned, and shook his head.

"Jesus, Mary and Joseph, will yer look at the size of them!" exclaimed O'Brien.

P.C. Kelsey's eyes widened, even he could see that the six foot silver bullets with tail propellers were torpedoes. Two of them. The ordinance was duly loaded onto 'The Feisty Lady'. Each pipe was primed with its rocket and the torpedoes were slid into their tubes, port and starboard.

"We should arrest them now!" said P.C. Kelsey.

"We need to catch them in the act," said Inspector O'Brien.

"Looks feckin' dangerous to me," said P.C. Kelsey.

"I agree, Patrick," said the Inspector, "the police boat is in dry dock we'll have to requisition the lifeboat and get it loaded onto a trailer pronto and then follow this little feckin' circus wherever it goes."

To Inspector O'Brien's delight his request was carried out to the letter. In less than three hours the hard inflatable twin screw orange lifeboat was hooked up to O'Brien's Mercedes Sprinter. Two burly members of the lifeboat crew, Mick and Montmorency were there to assist the policemen. Four lifejackets were provided as well as two sub machine guns and magazine clips. Both Inspector O'Brien and P.C. Kelsey had been weapons trained. (P.C. Kelsey passed on the fourth attempt.)

It was obvious to D.I. Kendall that Brendan McHugh and his mob were making there way south in 'Zeppellin' sailing along the River Shannon and the intervening lochs. Local banks close to this watercourse were duly taking in the counterfeit punts and issuing kosher Euros in return. D.I. Kendall reckoned they would get all the way to Limerick eventually. He wanted to track 'Zeppellin' as far as the lower reaches of Loch Derg before confronting McHugh and informing The Garda.

"Why wait Steve?" implored Sergeant Broadbent.

"I want that slag McHugh and his mates to have Euros up to the gunwales. I want them to think that they've got away with the biggest heist in Irish history, and I want to nail the bastards when they think they've eventually pulled it off. Besides, I quite fancy doing a spot of fishing too, don't you John?"

Sgt. Broadbent groaned as he drove the trailer and 'Leprechaun' to Ballykeeran where they launched her into Loch Ree.

Two hours later, while happily fishing, they caught sight of 'Zeppellin' gliding down the loch. D.I. Kendall smiled broadly.

The fifth and final day of 'The Irish Match' would be held on Loch Derg. European funding at 95% with the Irish government chipping in with 5% had transformed Loch Derg into a fisherman's paradise. Along the southern shore of the loch a huge semi-circular boardwalk had been built, from which, at regular intervals sprouted 40 wooden platforms. Each platform was a 10m finger pointing into the loch and the distance between each platform was 25m. This gave each individual fisherman a huge area of the loch to fish independently. The first 36 platforms were the competitors' pegs for the final match. Platforms 37 to 40 were given to Sky Sports who had sole rights to the final match, live. Sky had already erected a crane with a cradle for the main cameraman on platform 40. Sky had left locked containers on the other three platforms containing outside broadcasting gear to be used on the final day.

Kathleen Connolly had arrived at Loch Derg's car park at 2am in the morning on the day of the final match. She had driven there on Martha D'Arcy's powerful Yamaha motorcycle, the lights of which she now switched off. The moon was up and it was a cool clear night. She left her helmet on the seat of the Yamaha and slung a knapsack over her left shoulder. What looked like motorcycle leathers was actually a dry suit which more than did justice to her voluptuous figure now silhouetted in the early morning moonlight.

She slid down the bank into the dark still waters of Loch Derg and waded out to the wooden stanchions at the end of platform 1. The water lapped just below her ample bosom. She had a head torch and around her neck a chain with a stapler attached.

From her knapsack she took the first of 36 plastic boxes each about the size of a cigarette packet. Each box contained a dollop of semtex, a detonator and a pre-programmed electronic switch.

Under the light of her head torch she stapled the box to the wooden stanchion and then hooked 2mm low-resistance copper wire through the trigger of the switch. She then moved on to platform 2 carefully unwinding the copper wire from a coil to be connected to the next switch trigger. The whole process was repeated on platform 2 and, painstakingly right up to and including platform 36, where the last of the copper wire was attached to the last electronic switch. It was old technology but nonetheless effective.

Kathleen smiled knowingly at her work. She had programmed each detonation to occur at two second intervals.

"Seventy two seconds of delicious mayhem all caught on camera thanks to Sky," she said to herself and chuckled.

It was 5:30am when Kathleen Connolly roared out of the Loch Derg car park feeling light headed and elated.

Chapter 14

It was the fourth day of 'The Irish Match', as everyone called it now. The four team members were all up early as it was a fair drive to Battlebridge and the River Boyle.

Sid had been singing all morning, mainly Beatles songs, he really did have a good singing voice it was just a pity that his breath stank. Nonetheless, Sid was an excellent 'river' man and the Boyle was his favourite. He knew he would do well, as did his colleagues.

It was a cloudy but warm day with a light breeze, ideal for river fishing and all four of them were upbeat about their prospects. They had all fished the stretch of river allocated for the match before, and were confident that they would do well on whatever peg they drew. There was no need to talk tactics.

Bernadette wobbled into the breakfast room with four steaming mugs of strong tea on a tray.

"There you go boys," she said "your breakfasts will follow." She gave Jonah a suggestive wink. Jonah smiled knowingly at Sid and Dave. A full Irish breakfast followed with a mountain of toast, which was enjoyed by all.

The Ford Transit was loaded. Rowley was the designated driver. Dave hauled the bait from the fridge. They would mainly be using casters and needlethread worms, ideal for catching bream and roach. It was Dave's turn to sit in the back. Sid squeezed in next to Rowley.

"Fancy an extra-strong mint, Sid?" asked Rowley.

"Not after a brekkie like that," said Sid, then "ey up Jonah get yer arse in 'ere, we're off!"

Jonah sidled up next to Bernadette on the doorstep and squeezed the left cheek of her pendulous arse.

"Tonight's the night gel," he whispered.

"Oh, and you're a devil of a man Jonah Carter," whispered Bernadette as her labia twitched with expectation and her heart raced. Jonah jumped into the Transit laughing, pulled on his balaclava and shades and off they sped.

The draw was a bit tricky. Charlie Hoskins had drawn peg 9. Next to him was Rowley on peg 10, and Jonah was on 11. Jonah's concentration kept lapsing as he considered that his nemesis was only two pegs down. He kept missing bites. Even so, towards the end of the match, he had a decent haul of bream, roach and skimmers in his keepnet.

Charlie Hoskins had hooked into a large bream and was playing it well until the bank gave way under his left foot and he fell sideways. He hung on to his rod and didn't lose the bream but his bait tray with all his bait had fallen into the river and had been swept away.

"Fack me rigid!" he exclaimed, as he lifted the bream into his landing net and then transferred it to his keepnet.

"I got no fackin' bait left!"

There was just over twenty minutes of the match left and the rest of his team were miles away on high numbered pegs.

"Would you Adam and Eve it!"

Hoskins was distraught but he had managed to rescue one bait box so he decided he'd ask the bloke on peg 10 if he could scrounge some hook bait for the remainder of the match. He scurried up river to peg 10. Rowley had a very lively perch on his hook and was obviously having trouble playing it.

"Mustn't bully the fish," he murmured.

"Fack that!" exclaimed Hoskins, and scuttled off to peg11.

Jonah was patiently waiting for a bite.

"Ere mate," called out Hoskins "doan 'appen to have a few spare casters do yer? I've kicked all me fackin' bait into the drink!"

Jonah froze and choked. He knew it was Charlie Hoskins.

"Oi, you wiv the balaclava, are you Mutt and Geoff or what!"

Jonah was catatonic. He couldn't speak.

"Can I help?" asked Rowley. Salvation!!

"Jus wanna few casters, I've lost all me bait," and pointing to Jonah "wots up wiv' im in the balaclava?"

"Oh, that's just John. Not been too well lately, head cold and laryngitis," and Rowley then lowered his voice and said quietly, "John's not the sharpest knife in the drawer, if you get my drift?"

"Got yer squire," and Charlie winked.

"Come on I've got plenty of casters and threadworms if you like."

"Blindin'!" exclaimed a grateful Charlie Hoskins. Jonah's heart was hammering in his chest, the sweat pouring down his face. He closed his eyes and breathed deeply.

"Charlie-fackin-Hoskins!" he thought.

He decided to tackle down, he couldn't concentrate now anyway. Clumsily he let his keepnet slip and he lost more than half of what was a 70lb bag of fish.

"Oh bollocks," he said "what a fackin' disaster!"

Jonah had had a fraught day on the River Boyle. He hadn't fished particularly well and he'd lost half his catch. The cheeks of his arse were still involuntarily clenching as he recalled the Charlie Hoskins incident.

"Fack me that was close, thank Christ for Rowley."

The team had decided to have an early night prior to the last day of the match on Loch Derg. Due mainly to Jonah's mishap, their team was now in second place, 8lb behind MID(i). They were confident, however, that they could pull off a win. They had all fished Loch Derg before and had always bagged up big style. Rowley Dave and Sid were at Mary's bar under strict instructions to only have a couple of drinks. Jonah didn't join them he had to remain fully alcohol free and organize his plan to send Bernadette into orgasmic overdrive.

By 9:30pm the they were all back at their digs. Rowley made himself a steaming cup of cocoa and beetled off to bed. Jonah spoke to Sid and Dave.

"Now boys," said Jonah, "you sure you're up to this?"

Sid, who already had a rock solid erection, said he was.

"The picture will be there won't it?" asked Dave.

"Yes my son," assured Jonah.

"Should be okay then," said Dave.

As Bernadette tinkered about in the kitchen, Jonah stole into her bedroom and blue-tacked a picture of a huge carp on the wall of her bedroom just above the head board.

Bernadette was at the sink, washing up. Jonah crept up behind her and cupped her enormous baps in his hands, tweaking her nipples erect. Bernadette dropped the plate she was washing back into the sink and moaned softly. The man in her boat throbbed, and an instantly secreted rivulet of gelatinous minge juice wet her knickers.

Bernadette closed her eyes and swayed gently. Jonah's hot breath was in her left ear.

"Are you ready for this gel?" and Jonah pressed her hand against his erect pork sabre which was warmly throbbing in his jockey shorts.

"Oh, Jonah, 'tis a terrible man you are, oh Mary and Joseph I feel dizzy!"

Bernadette gasped her way upstairs hurriedly disrobed and lay in her bed dreamily looking at a picture of a huge carp.

"Know the drill?" Jonah asked Sid and Dave who, both clad only in dressing gowns, nodded in the affirmative.

"Here we go then," said Jonah.

Eamon and Liam Duff were back in business. Despite their appalling mishap, they still retained the license to transport used and dyed punts to Dublin for incineration.

And now they had another Transit van. It was better than their original, which they had inadvertently blown to bits. They only had to rustle up a mere 75 Euros to put to their 400 Euro windfall to purchase it.

They couldn't afford to have their name and logo professionally painted on the sides of the van, so Eamon did it instead. On both sides in gold paint Eamon had emblazoned the legend 'DUFF SECKURITY' 'by apointment to the Irish Govenment'.

"It doesn't look right," said Liam.

"'Tis the Irish spelling," said Eamon, who had long since realized his spelling errors but couldn't be arsed to paint it all out and start again.

Liam was made up with the van and continually boasted to his mates that "it can do over a hundred!" What he didn't tell them was the vans maximum speed was just over 100kph which, in old money, was only 63mph.

Nonetheless, they had three banks to call at the following day. One at Athlone, one at Nenagh, a small town near the picturesque Loch Derg, and one at Limerick. Finally they would take the road and their cargo to Dublin.

Chapter 15

Jonah slipped into bed beside the heavily breathing Bernadette.

"Why the fish picture?" she wheezed.

"Inspiration my love," replied Jonah.

"Oh, I see," said Bernadette, who didn't see at all.

Jonah kissed and fondled the nubile Bernadette who, clutching his ram rod mega-donger in both hands, urged him to 'get on with it!'

"Here's the plan," said Jonah.

"The plan?" gasped Bernadette.

Jonah threw all the bedclothes off the bed and instructed Bernadette to lay belly-down arse-up with her head on three pillows.

"Doggy-style," said Jonah, "now you keep your head buried in those pillows until you come. Understand?"

"I do, oh yes I do!"

"Okay then, here we go."

Jonah gripped Bernadette's hips and eased his nine-incher between her moist flaps. He started slowly, a full penetration every two seconds.

"Oh, Jesus, Mary, and Joseph!" gasped Bernadette.

Sid was standing by the bedroom door which was slightly ajar. His nose and most of his erect dick were the only parts of his anatomy actually inside the bedroom.

Jonah picked up the rhythm. A stroke every second now.

"Go on, go on, oh go on, ah, ah!"

Jonah kept this going for fully 15 minutes before stepping up the stroke to two every second.

Sid smiled. He was impressed.

"Oh, oh, oh, oh, ooo, ooo, ah, oh, go on, oh!"

Another ten minutes passed before Jonah went in to overdrive and banged away at Bernadette at three stokes a second!

"Go on, go on, nearly, nearly, oh Mother Superior, go on, nearly there, go on!"

After a further ten minutes, Jonah creamed his cocoa and tipped a wink to Sid.

Jonah slithered down Bernadette kissing her neck, back, bum, thigh, calf, ankles, toes, and, seamlessly Sid kissed Bernadette's toes, ankles, calf, thigh, bum, back and neck and then slipped his own offering into her honeypot!

"Oh, oh, oh, go on, go on, don't stop, go on, oh!" Amid the delirium, and for a fraction of a second, Bernadette was faintly aware of a whiff of bad breath which hardly bothered her.

"Oh Jonah, go on, go on, go on, oh, oh, oh!"

Bernadette was also aware that Jonah had changed his technique.

Sid was in fact a long-stroke man. The outstroke would just expose the collar of his bell and the instroke would pound Bernadette's pubis. This invariably pushed several cubic centimetres of air into Bernadette, who now accompanied every stroke from Sid with a sonorous minge-fart. She cared not a jot.

"Go on, go on, go on, nearly there, oh go on, oh, oh!"

Dave looked on through the partially open bedroom door. He still only had a partial erection.

Sid had been going a good twenty minutes and he was now riding Bernadette like a stallion.

"Oh, ah, oh, ah, oh, aaaahh, go on, go on, nearly, oh go on!"

Sid added his own juice to the interior of Bernadette's vagina which was now at 'bill poster's bucket' consistency.

"Ah, ah, ah, ah, yes, yes, oh yes, go on, go on, go on!"

Sid waved to Dave and slid out of Bernadette kissing her neck, back, bum, thigh, calf, foot and toes. Dave did the same in reverse, and as soon as he saw the picture of the huge carp he became ramrod stiff and pushed his pecker into Bernadette.

"Oh go on, go on, don't stop, go on, oh yes, oh, oh!"

Dave was a 'stop-start man'. He would give Bernadette six rapid strokes, then stop for an instant, take a deep breath, then give her another six rapid strokes.

"Oh the darling man is trying everything he knows!" thought Bernadette, who truly believed she was on course to go over the edge.

"Oh, go on Jonah, go on, ah, ah, ah, yes, yes, oh, go on!"

Jonah dispatched the 50mg Viagra tablet with a swig of single malt Scotch whisky, and while Dave was still spanking Bernadette's flaps, his monolithic appendage surged with blood and, once again, became a solid rod.

Dave had done well. Bernadette's tone had changed and had become even more frantic.

"Yes, oh yes, yes, yes, nearly there, this is it, oh yes, go on, oh go on!"

The conjugal change over between Dave and Jonah was as seamless as the others.

Jonah knew his drug-induced erection was good for some twenty minutes. He immediately started off at a frenetic pace.

"Oh, oh, oh, yes, yes, yes, go on, go on, ahhh, yes, go on!"

Energy, heat, sweat, steam, fanny juice, minge farts were everywhere in a maelstrom of coital industry.

"Yes, oh yes, oh yes, oh, oh, aahh, go on, this is it!"

Fifteen minutes later Jonah felt as though his todger had become fully desensitized and for a minute or so he felt defeat gnawing away at his ego.

He gave Bernadette the most frantic five minutes he had ever performed and then suddenly . . . hallelujah!

"YES, YES, OH YES, YES, YES, YES, AAAAHHHGG GHH, OH, YEEEESSSSSSS!!!"

Bernadette's insides convulsed in the most cataclysmic orgasm.

"AAAHHHHHHHHHHHHHHHHHGGGGGGGGGG, YEEEEEEEEEEEESSSSSSSSSSSSSSS!!!"

Four local dogs within earshot howled at the moon, and three car alarms went off!

Jonah punched the air and whooped victoriously. Dave and Sid stood, unashamedly, stark-bollock-naked in the bedroom doorway and applauded Jonah enthusiastically.

Bernadette was oblivious to it all and, in a state of post-orgasmic delirium drifted into a deep sleep with a smile on her face.

The first of the 36 fishermen (and women) arrived at around 7am and looked out over the beautiful Loch Derg. It was a bright clear morning, the Loch a millpond.

The 'Sky Sports' boys had arrived at about the same time. There would be three 'roving' reporters, interviewing the fishermen individually during the match with the main camera in situ in the cradle at the top of the crane on platform 40. The cameraman here had a panoramic view of the event and the loch, as well as being able to zoom in on every fisherman from platform 1 to 36.

The bailiffs arrived next with the dignitaries from the sponsors, Daiwa Rods and Shimano Reels, who, after the match was finished, would award the winning team 100,000 Euros in a well televised ceremony. This would be the biggest prize ever given to an angling event, hence the huge T.V. coverage.

NW(i) arrived in Jonah's Ford Transit at 7:45am and unloaded all their gear onto their trolleys in the car park. They had said a fond farewell to Bernadette as they were heading home straight after the final match. All the other teams were there by now. The draw would be at 8:15. The match would start at 9:00am.

Jonah shifted uneasily. He wore his balaclava and his eyes behind his shades searched for Charlie Hoskins. Rowley spotted his distress.

"Calm down lad," he said "I've put Hoskins off the scent all you have to do is act like a moron."

"Thanks Rowley," said Jonah sarcastically.

There was a nice touch at the draw which NW(i) really appreciated. None other than Karen Stoker, Ladies European Champion and team captain of MID(i), who were the current leaders, had a cheery word with them.

"I know it will be close lads, after all there's only 8lb in it, but, all the best anyway," and she shook hands with all four team members and wished them well.

"Nice lady," said Rowley, "stonking tits!" he thought.

"And a brilliant angler," added Dave.

Jonah had drawn peg 2, next to him was Billy Suggs of SE(ii) on 3. Luckily, Charlie Hoskins was on peg 28 and well out of the way.

"Thank Christ," thought Jonah.

"All in!" and at 9am the final match was underway.

Chapter 16

D.I. Kendall and Sgt Broadbent, in their rust bucket 'Leprechaun' had stalked Brendan McHugh and Mick Kelly in 'Zeppellin' across Loch Ree and down the River Shannon into Loch Derg.

Although, technically 'Leprechaun' was a motor sailor of sorts, it only had a moth-eaten mainsail which D.I. Kendall had left in its mildewed bag. There was bugger all wind anyway.

He would have to rely on the inboard engine, an ancient Perkins diesel, which had been spluttering alarmingly for the past couple of hours. 'Leprechaun' had also sprung a leak and the bilges were almost full before Sgt Broadbent spotted the problem and switched the bilge pumps on. The pumps were as ancient as the engine but Sgt Broadbent had ascertained that they were pumping out water at a very slightly quicker rate than the leak was letting in.

"Don't know how long these bilge pumps are gonna last boss," said Broadbent.

"Or the fucking engine for that matter John," said a gloomy D.I. Kendall.

Just then 'Zeppellin' anchored.

"Okay John, I'll switch the engine and pumps off, give them a rest. You use the bucket to bail out the bilges and I'll pretend to do a bit of fishing."

"Okay, boss."

So 'Leprechaun' was anchored up as D.I. Kendall simulated fishing whilst keeping an eye on 'Zeppellin'. Sgt Broadbent bailed out the bilges at a considerably faster rate than the pumps had managed, but the leak was getting worse.

Brendan McHugh scanned the lower reaches of the Loch with his binoculars.

"Just as I thought," he said.

"Thought what?" asked Mick Kelly.

"'Tis a feckin' big prestigious fishing match on the loch. Loads of barmy Englishmen, watched over by Sky TV, no less. Twill be all over by 2:30pm, so we can move in then and make the final drop."

"Right!" enthused Kelly.

In the cockpit of 'Zeppellin' were six huge heavy duty blue bags stuffed with brand new Euros and two red bags containing the last of the counterfeit Punts.

Martha D'Arcy, dressed in battle fatigues, jumped in beside Kathleen Connolly who drove the Range Rover, hooked up to 'The Feisty Lady', out of the grounds of D'Arcyfields.

"Don't worry about being spotted, stay quite close to them," said Inspector O'Brien.

"Why's that then?" asked P.C. Kelsey.

"We're towin' a feckin' lifeboat, not a police boat. It's not suspicious."

"Is it not?" asked P.C. Kelsey.

"Oh shut yer gob, and drive!"

Kelsey eased through the gears of the Mercedes Sprinter. The lifeguards, Mick and Montmorency were in the back.

Kathleen Connolly backed the trailer down a slipway on the north-east shore of Loch Derg, and 'The Feisty Lady' was duly launched. It was 12:30pm.

"The party will start at 1 o'clock," said Martha D'Arcy to her colleague.

"Are you sure you want to do this alone, Martha, I'll willingly come with you," said Kathleen.

"I've nothing to lose," said Martha, "but you have a fine man and a close knit family."

Kathleen knew Martha was right and besides, the eventual outcome would invariably lead to imprisonment which she couldn't stomach again.

"God speed Martha. This is for FOIF!" declared Kathleen.

"Indeed," replied a pensive Martha, "goodbye Kathleen." The comrades embraced.

Kathleen Connolly pushed 'The Feisty Lady' away from the shoreline and Martha fired up the powerful Volvo engines and slowly motored off.

P.C. Kelsey backed the trailer along the rocky edge of Loch Derg's north shore. Mick and Montmorency easily launched the lifeboat and, after he had parked the Mercedes Sprinter in the car park, P.C. Kelsey joined the other three men in the lifeboat. All four men put on life jackets. Mick would steer. Montmorency would be lookout.

Inspector O'Brien opened his rucksack and took out a loudhailer and two sub-machine guns. He pointed to the guns.

"Only in an emergency and only to scare her, or to hole her boat," he said.

P.C. Kelsey regarded the guns, a stern expression on his face. "Is the 'safety' on?"

"'Tis," replied O'Brien, then, "okay Mick steady as she goes, let's see what this demented Englishwoman is up to."

Montmorency fired up one of the huge Mercury outboards and Mick steered the craft slowly into the loch.

"This leaks getting worse, Steve," said Sgt Broadbent.

"Okay, John, I'll turn the pumps on."

The bilge pumps lasted twenty seconds before they packed up for good.

"Oh, Christ!" said D.I. Kendall, "you got your mobile John, I left mine in the car?"

Broadbent passed over his mobile phone.

"Who you phoning?" he said.

"Branch of The Garda, Irish Intelligence," said Steve, "I've had their number for weeks, got it from The Met. I'll clue them up and then we're out of here before we sink."

Kendall switched on the mobile phone. It bleeped and registered 'Low Battery' on the screen. He quickly punched in the eleven digit number. The phone rang for an eternity and then an Irish voice said, "Code and Number."

"Aztec zero four four zero," replied Kendall.

"Good," said Irish Intelligence, then the line went dead.

"Hells bells!" shouted Kendall.

The 'Irish Match' was approaching the final hour.

'All out!' would be called at 2pm.

All members of NW(i) had caught well. Dave Tonks was filling up his SECOND keepnet! The roving reporters had moved along the platforms quietly interviewing the competitors. Rowley was one of the chosen ones. He would review it later as his wife Trish was recording the match coverage from Sky Sports.

One of the mobile cameramen had tried to interview Dave Tonks, but to no avail, nothing could break his intense concentration.

"Suit yourself," said the cameraman who shrugged his shoulders and moved on to the next platform.

Dave would be mentioned in dispatches, however, as it became obvious to the cameraman in the cradle that the bloke on platform 17 (i.e. Dave Tonks) had probably caught twice as many fish as any of the other 35 competitors. NW(i) were on course to win 'The Irish Match' hands down.

Chapter 17

It was 1pm. Martha D'Arcy throttled back in 'The Feisty Lady', some 100m from the fishing platforms. She switched on her loudhailer.

"THIS IS THE FRIENDS OF IRISH FISH, FOIF!!" she exclaimed. "IT IS A PROVEN SCIENTIFIC FACT THAT FISH HAVE A LOW THRESHOLD OF PAIN. IT IS ALSO A FACT THAT MANY IRISH FISH HAVE BEEN INJURED AND DEFORMED BY THE USE OF BARBED HOOKS!"

"What the deuce is all this about?" mused Rowley, "we only ever use barbless hooks."

Martha continued. "YOU ENGLISHMEN ARE NOT WELCOME HERE, PUT ALL THE FISH BACK INTO THE LOCH NOW AND GO HOME! THIS MIGHT HELP YOU MAKE UP YOUR MIND!"

Martha fired off all six pipe rockets which exploded in the loch some 50m from the platforms.

"Fat lot of good that will do your Irish fish you maniac!" shouted Rowley.

The explosive force from the pipe rockets had set up a tsunami with a long rolling wave some 2m in height which moved inexorably towards the platforms.

"Right Mick!" said Inspector O'Brien, "cut across her prow, a little bow wave might unsettle her. Patrick, fire off a few warning shots!"

As P.C. Kelsey fired off half a magazine into the air, Inspector O'Brien picked up his loudhailer.

"THIS IS THE POLICE! MARTHA D'ARCY YOU ARE UNDER ARREST. CUT YOUR ENGINES WE ARE COMING TO BOARD YOU!"

"FUCK OFF!" was Martha's eloquent reply.

"Oooo," said Montmorency, "not very ladylike is she Mick, dear?"

The lifeboat cut a swathe in front of 'The Feisty Lady' which rocked sideways. Martha D'Arcy, with the lifeboat in her sights, discharged the port torpedo.

"Fuck me, we're out of here!" said D.I. Kendall, who turned the ignition on but 'Leprechaun's' engine was dead.

Lifeguard Mick caught sight of the torpedo and he steered violently to starboard to avoid it. The torpedo skimmed the stern of the lifeboat and detonated with awesome force into the hull of 'Zeppellin'.

Brendan McHugh and Mick Kelly were blown some 8m into the air and, although he felt no pain, Mick Kelly noticed that his left leg had gone AWOL. Then he caught a glimpse of it sailing through the air together with 6 blue bags 2 red bags and sundry bits of 'Zeppellin'.

"There's me place in the team gone!" Mick Kelly thought morosely. (He played football for Athlone Athletic. Left back.)

The blast which blew 'Zeppellin' to smithereens also ripped a huge hole into the side of 'Leprechaun' which sank like a brick, and two bewildered British coppers swam frantically ashore.

The tsunami hit the platforms. All the competitors were drenched and the force of the wave swept away most of their tackle and keepnets.

Jonah ripped off his shades and soggy balaclava and threw them disgustedly down onto his platform now awash with debris.

"You stupid fackin' cow!" he bawled at Martha.

Charlie Hoskins had just arrived on platform 3 to see how Billy Suggs was doing and to dog a packet of size 16 hooks off him. He recognized Jonah instantly.

"You fackin' toerag Carter!!" and, knife in hand, Hoskins made a beeline for Jonah.

"Got to try and dodge round him," Jonah thought frantically. If he could just get past Charlie Hoskins, Jonah knew he could outrun him. He picked up his Swiss army knife and waited for the imminent assault.

Kathleen Connolly pressed the 'send' button on her mobile phone.

As Charlie Hoskins thundered down platform 2 intent on disemboweling Jonah Carter, platform 1 exploded and collapsed into the loch together with its terrified tenant.

Charlie Hoskins stopped in his tracks, and two seconds later platform 2 exploded.

Charlie was blown back landing headfirst on the asphalt walkway. He was knocked unconscious. Carter was deposited in a reed bed on the side of the loch.

"YOU FECKIN' MANIAC!!" yelled Inspector O'Brien into his loudhailer, "STOP NOW OR WE SHOOT TO KILL!!"

With that he fired a complete magazine towards the hull of 'The Feisty Lady'.

Martha D'Arcy swung her craft round and fired her starboard torpedo. 'The Feisty Lady' was listing to port as the torpedo was jettisoned. Like a flat stone, the torpedo skimmed across the surface of the water. It clipped the prow of the lifeboat and became airborne flying towards the road.

The torpedo cut a hole in the offending 'K' of the 'Duff Seckurity' van and exploded! The van split into two. The rear became a fireball of Irish punts. Eamon and Liam Duff, wide-eyed and petrified hung on to each other as the cabin flew some 5m off the ground, eventually coming to a juddering halt in a peat bog.

"I'm done with this feckin' business!" exclaimed Liam, and then, "whoa, what's that awful stink!"

"I've shit meself," said Eamon.

After the fifth platform exploded it became obvious to all the fishermen that they were being detonated in sequence. EXODUS!! Thirty-odd fishermen bounded off to the car park, leapt into their vans, and drove off manically. SE(ii) were one of the last teams to flee the debacle as Billy Suggs had to drag an unconscious Charlie Hoskins all the way to their van.

Rowley, Dave and Sid piled into their Transit.

"Where's Jonah?" asked Sid.

"Don't know," said Rowley, "but he's okay."

"But . . ." started Dave, Rowley cut him short.

"Put a sock in it lad, we're out of here!"

Jonah was moving stealthily through the reed bed, as the other fishermen were racing for their vans, when he came across two curious objects. One looked like a human leg. The other was a huge blue bag. Jonah still had his Swiss Army knife in his hand so he cut into the bag.

"Lovely jubbly!" he said, and then sent Rowley a text.

Epilogue

Fergal O'Shaunessy, the man with the brilliant hands, spent his ill-gotten money on gallons of Bushmills whiskey and loose women. He died a happy man. Colin the flea died with him.

Father McCartney gave up the cloth, became a pub singer, and discovered the joys of sex. He married a sixteen year old colleen who, after one year, presented him with twin girls making him a real father at last.

Kelly 'The Kraut' Gruntfahrt was named 'Irishman of The Millennium' and was given a medallion and certificate to prove it.

Martha D'Arcy was given 9 years and was allowed to serve her sentence in Holloway Women's Prison in England. The Irish were pleased to see the back of her.

D.I. Kendall and Sgt Broadbent were both busted down to police constables for working outside their jurisdiction. They promptly resigned and set up a private investigation agency. 'S and J's Eyes', Broadbent's idea.

Inspector Kieran O'Brien was promoted to Chief Inspector and P.C. Patrick Kelsey became a sergeant.

Mick and Montmorency became husband and husband at a civil ceremony in Croydon England.

Charlie Hoskins eventually recovered consciousness to find he had amnesia. He didn't even recognize his missus who promptly divorced him.

Kathleen Connolly married her fine man and opened up a B&B in Limerick.

Mick Kelly got a new leg and both he and Brendan McHugh got 6 years apiece in the local nick.

Eamon and Liam Duff used their insurance payout, (thank God they remembered to post it off this time), to purchase an ice cream van and opt for a safer lifestyle as Mr Fluffy and Mr Creamy.

Bernadette wore a perpetual smile these days. The aftermath of her mega-orgasm had radically changed her biology. Her internal erogenous zones, long since dormant, had woken up. Now, a mere five minute bonk would leave her on an ethereal plane of delicious multiple orgasms. She had no end of suitors but she eventually settled down with Rory McKiney, the recently widowed butcher from the adjacent village, from whom she got plenty of fresh meat.

Sky Sports TV had the sporting scoop of the century!
The mayhem at Loch Derg was even made into a DVD, which sold in its millions.

During the debacle, Rowley had received a text from Jonah.
'Go without me, don't worry, I'm okay. Be lucky.'
So Rowley, Dave and Sid had travelled back to Liverpool with hardly any of their expensive tackle and no winnings.

The sponsors eventually gave the winner's cheque, and the prestige, to the team who were in the lead after 4 days, MID(i).

Three weeks after the debacle, Jonah boarded a plane at Dublin Airport destined for Malaga Spain.

"Need a few months in the sun," he said to himself.

Before he left Jonah had posted three letters.

The Sting

Rowley, Dave and Sid each received a registered letter on the same day.

Each letter had the same contents, a personal banker's draft for £100,000, and a note.

"We did win after all. Be lucky!"

Author's Afterthought

No fish were harmed during the writing of this book.

Sadly, all the characters in this book are fictitious.
However, **some** of the events did actually happen!
Nice!

Authors Thanks

To Tom Sharpe and the late ("I told you I was ill!) Spike Milligan. Their books are an inspiration.

The end:

If you enjoyed reading this book may I recommend you read my first novel, 'Shenanigans' (at McGillchrist Hall) . . . a ripping yarn.